BROTHERS THREE

C.W. JAMES

INSUNDRY PRODUCTIONS
BOOKS

For information contact :
http://www.insundryproductions.com
Insundry Productions Books
Gardnerville, NV
Cover artwork by phanduy
ISBN (ebook): 978-1-7368013-6-9
ISBN (paperback): 978-1-7368013-5-2
Library of Congress Control Number: 2022912967

With thanks to
Ralph Bonehill, Edward Stratemeyer, or the ghost

Also by C.W. James
The Treasure of Peril Island

Chapter 1

The shotgun blasts rent the hot, still June air. A hawk, disturbed by the noise, took to wing, flying low on the thermals from the valley floor, complaining with its eerie cry.

Allen Winthrup reined in his horse and stood in the stirrups, automatically dropping one hand to the handle of his holstered Colt revolver. The empty, broad valley spread out around him, rimmed by mountains and capped by a blue, cloudless sky. He took off his hat and wiped the perspiration from his forehead with the sleeve of his shirt.

The sound of the shotgun could have been an echo from a distant fire or someone shooting at a rattlesnake. He waited for additional or answering shots. There were none, so perhaps the gunfire was a signal.

"That sounded like it could have come from our ranch," he said to his mare. He spurred her into a gallop. "Let's get home."

As Allen sped toward his spread, the various scenarios that could be awaiting him crowded his brain. It was possible that Paul or Chet had injured themselves in an accident or were sick. At least the lack of smoke on the horizon indicated that last summer's fire, which almost burned down their house, wasn't aflame again.

When his father died two years ago, Allen assumed the role of caretaker for his two younger brothers, although he was only fifteen at the time. After their father's death, their uncle, Barnaby, became their guardian and executor.

Another happier thought came to him: maybe his uncle had returned home.

As there was really little to do at the ranch but look after the cattle, Allen's restless uncle left the place in charge of the three boys while he continued month in and month out to range over the hills and among the mountains in search of precious metal, which lay concealed beneath the surface. One day, Allen's uncle staggered into the house with the news that he'd struck a bonanza. He refused to give more detail about its location, instead announcing his plan to travel to San Francisco to organize a company to work the claim. He set out on his trip a couple of months ago, apparently healthy, but the brothers hadn't seen him or heard from him since. They were used to Uncle Barnaby being out of contact for weeks at a time while prospecting, but never this long.

That must be it, Allen thought. Uncle Barnaby returned from Frisco with a bang, a gunshot in celebration. Allen shook his head and broke into a rare grin. Boy, was he going to give Uncle Barnaby hell for not writing to the family while he was in Frisco.

The distinctive neigh of his horse alerted Allen that he was nearly home. He crested the last hill, and the ranch came into view. The home sat on one of the numerous branches of the winding Salmon River, a site chosen by his father many years before. The house was a rough but comfortable dwelling, with barns and other outbuildings within close walking distance. Middle brother Paul stood waiting there in front, a shotgun in his hand.

Paul was tall, well-built, and, like Allen, had a tanned complexion from working on the ranch as he grew up. He shared the raven-black hair of his brothers, and it squirted on this forehead from under the brim of his hat as though trying to escape. Even after 15 years, though, Allen still couldn't quite figure out his younger sibling. He reminded Allen of the old saying he learned during his short stint in formal schooling: "still waters run deep." On the surface, Paul appeared calm and quiet, but Allen sensed he churned with turbulent emotions underneath.

"Hi, Allen! This way, quick!" Paul said, raising his voice.

"All right, Paul!" Allen called back as he dashed up on his faithful mare. He dismounted and gestured toward the shotgun. Paul returned a wry grin.

"Shooting this off was Chet's idea. He wanted to signal you if you were nearby." The smile disappeared and his brown eyes turned serious. "Allen, we've—"

Chet burst out of the barn, his blue shirt whipping behind him as if it had a mind of its own and his collar length hair bouncing. The fourteen-year-old boy was the shortest and smallest of the three. Muscles rippled under his skin, showed his surprising strength for his size. "Allen! Allen!" he shouted as he ran up. "Somebody stole our horses!"

Allen gave a low whistle and tilted back his hat, his eyes searching the ground, his hands on his hips. So much for hoping for good news. "Stolen! When? What happened?"

"We were—" Chet blurted out.

Paul turned to Chet and put one hand on his shoulder to calm him. "We just got back from the river," he continued in his deliberate way. "We spent the morning fishing at our favorite deep hole."

Allen nodded, shifting his lean frame from one foot to the other and back again.

"You know, the one near the roots of that clump of cottonwood trees," Chet put in.

"We were coming back," Paul went on in his slow, measured speech. "When Chet pointed toward the barn and asked if I left the door unlocked. I didn't, so I thought maybe you had come back."

"We started for the barn," Chet excitedly took up the story. "When we got inside, it was enough... it told everything... Jasper and Rush were gone."

"Any idea when this happened?" Allen asked.

"There's really no telling," responded Paul. "We just got back from the river a few minutes ago and found the barn door broken open and both horses gone. If I remember—we went off about eight o'clock this morning, didn't we, Chet?"

"Yes, around then."

"It's about noon now," said Paul. "So the thieves had four hours to do their dirty work. They were alone and unmolested."

Allen grunted a response, turned, and walked to the barn. Paul and Chet followed. The broken lock's brackets bent back, and it held no longer than a rag. Allen looked toward his brothers for answers.

"See how the lock and hasp is busted open," Chet pointed to the wrecked padlock.

Allen nodded and stepped into the barn, stopping just inside the door and waiting for his eyes to adjust to the light. Despite the situation, he welcomed the cool darkness of the interior.

"Thieves, as sure as fate!" Allen said, gazing around at every corner. "And they took all the extra harnesses as well."

"As sure as fate," repeated Chet, his black eyes flashing angrily. He waved a hand at the empty wall where the equipment was usually stored.

Allen shook his head in disgust. He paced around a little in front of it, thinking. "And no clues? Did either of you find anything?"

"No," Paul admitted. "We haven't had time to look."

"Let's search," Allen ordered. "We need more light in here."

Paul reached into his pocket and pulled out a waterproof box containing matches. He fished one out and struck it against a flint, lighting a kerosene lamp. He handed it to Allen. The three began searching.

"Here is a strap that isn't part of our outfit." Chet snatched it up, but quickly threw it back down. "But it's only a common affair that might belong to anyone. No help to us."

The trio continued to scour the barn.

"Well, hasn't anybody found something yet?" Allen demanded irritably.

"Wait! Here's a metal cross!" Chet announced as he picked it up out of a pile of dirt on the floor.

The article was in an 'X' shape, with a round hole drilled directly in the center. Each of the four corners contained one letter: DAFG.

"It could be made of silver, but so unpolished you can't tell." Paul bent over to examine the cross as it lay in his brother's hand. "What do you make of it?"

Chet shrugged. "Nothing more than a metal cross with letters on it. I've never seen one like it before."

"Is there no name on that thing?" Paul touched the cross.

Chet quickly flipped the cross over and moved to the open door for more light. Some letters were carved in the metal crudely, as if with a knife. "S. M.," read Chet, slowly. "I wonder who they stand for?"

"Sam somebody, I suppose." Paul shrugged.

"Whoever they are, they must be mean enough to turn a horse thief," Chet growled.

Allen grabbed the silver cross out of Chet's hand. "Let me see it."

"Hey!" protested Chet.

Allen turned the item over in his hands once. He looked like he was about to speak, but stopped short and muttered something under his breath.

"You know what that is?" Paul asked Allen. "Do you recognize it?"

"No, but Pa told me about it once," said Allen. "It's an old Sol Davids gang cross they wore. DAFG: Dare All For Gold! That was their old motto."

"So it follows the horse thieves might be some left-overs from the old outfit," noted Paul.

"Yes, they are most likely of the same bad crowd, a remnant of the outlaw band from Jordan Creek. I figured they would spring up again, sooner or later," said Allen. "The hanging of old Sol didn't drive them out of this district as folks had hoped."

"But what of the initials S. M.?" wondered Chet. "I never heard of any horse thief those would fit."

"We'll find out about that when we run the thieves down," said Allen. "Let's take a look around, and see if we can't find some other clue to their identity."

The brothers resumed their careful search.

"You say you discovered the robbery but a short while since?" Allen clarified after a few minutes.

"Not more than a quarter of an hour ago," replied Chet.

"Either of you been up to the house?"

"I went for my gun, so we could signal you," began Chet. "We figured if you were near enough—" he started, and then meeting his older brother's eyes, he stopped short.

Not one of the three said a word for a moment. They all tore out of the barn, with Chet leading the way. In record time, they burst through the front door of the house, and stood there, panting.

"Looks like everything is all right ... " began Paul.

"No, it is not!" yelled Chet, leaping forward. "The side window has been forced open."

Allen glanced at it, but said nothing. He continued to his sleeping room, which used to be his parents' room, and opened the door. It was a shambles: the bedclothes on the floor; drawers pulled out of the dresser; his clothes thrown about everywhere. He began to dig through the mess, into a closet and two trunks. He let out an angry curse and slammed his fist against the wall. His brothers crowded into the doorway, looking at him anxiously.

"What's going on?" they asked in unison.

"Everything's gone," said Allen in a hoarse voice.

"Gone?" gasped Chet.

"Yes," said Allen, "all our savings for years! Seven hundred dollars, plus three bags of silver and gold! We've been cleaned out."

Paul and Chet groaned.

"They must have started in your room," Paul said, "and when they found the stash, they figured they got it all and left. It looks like they didn't bother to search the rest of the house at all."

"The mean, contemptible scoundrels!" Allen swore. "We must get after them somehow!"

Chet frowned. "How? We're tied fast here. We can't follow on foot—they knew that when they came to rob us and took the horses."

"You are not going to sit down and suck your thumb again, are you, Chet?" Allen spat out.

"What do you mean by that remark? We can't do anything! We must go for the sheriff!" Chet fired back.

Allen shook his head. "It would take at least a day to travel to town and bring back the law. The thieves' trail would be cold by then, and they would be scattered to the four winds—with your horses and the money."

"Now who's sitting down and sucking his thumb, Allen?" Chet challenged.

"Allen's right, Chet," said Paul. He addressed his big brother. "What do you have in mind?"

"I'll go after them," decided Allen with swift determination. "I have my horse. I'll get my rifle. I already have my pistol."

"You are not going alone, are you?" asked Paul, concerned.

"There is no choice. There is only my mare to be had—mine."

"That can be foolhardy, Allen," cautioned Paul. "What could one fellow do against two or more? They would knock you over at the first opportunity."

"I won't give them the chance," countered Allen grimly. "As they used to say when Pa was young, I'll shoot first and talk afterward."

"If you're going, I'm going with you," Chet asserted.

Allen shook his head. "No."

"Two of us can ride on Lily. I don't weigh much, certainly less than Paul," Chet argued.

Allen shook his head again. "No, it can't be done, Chet; not with her all tired out after her morning's trip."

"But Allen—" Chet started.

"I'm going alone. You are to stay here," Allen declared.

"You can't—" Chet tried again.

"No, Chet, that's final. I gave you an order," Allen commanded.

"Order? An order! Who do you think you are to give orders?" Chet bristled. "You don't inherit your share of the ranch until you turn 18. Until then, Uncle Barnaby is our guardian."

"In case you didn't notice, our uncle isn't here now, so you will do as I say!" Allen shot back. "I'm still the eldest and still in charge."

"Just because you're the oldest, you think that gives you the right—" Chet shouted.

"That's enough, both of you," Paul interjected sharply, but still in his usual soft-spoken tone. The effect was as instant as dumping water on two fighting cats. Allen and Chet fell silent for a moment.

"Maybe the trail will pass by another ranch, and then I'll call on the neighbors for help," Allen offered after a pause. "I promise I won't tackle the thieves on my own."

"Can you follow their tracks?" questioned Paul.

"I think so. At least, I'll try. They won't get far if they leave the river, but it doesn't seem like they'll do that," Allen answered.

Allen slipped into the main room of the house, went to the gun cabinet, and retrieved his Winchester. He headed out the front door, Chet and Paul behind. With a curt nod towards them, Allen mounted his horse. A few minutes later, he was off in the pursuit of the thieves. The dust clouds kicked up by Lily rose up in his wake like smoke from a growing fire.

Allen moved down the trail until the buildings of the ranch were far behind. He knew this way well, and it was easy to find the tracks—the new ones made by the hoofs of four horses.

"As long as they remain as fresh as they are now, it will be simple enough to follow them," he said to Lily, patting her on the side. He urged her forward over the rough terrain in a way that displayed his affection for the animal, while also revealing his reluctance to make her work more than she could reasonably bear.

After moving through the belt of cottonwood trees, Allen reached a small stream that flowed into the river a little farther on. He looked around at his surroundings and paused to examine the signs on the wet bank.

The thieves probably came quite a distance to reach the ranch, he reasoned, so they must have needed to water their horses. That means they would most likely go back a long way before they'd settle down for the night.

"Heigh-ho!" he said aloud as he got off the ground. "I'm afraid a long and difficult search stretches before us, Lily."

The tracks on the far side suggested that the robbers forded the brook upstream, so Allen crossed over likewise, and five minutes later reached a bit of rolling land dotted with sagebrush and other bushes. He wondered if this was where the trail would lead; perhaps to Gold Fork, a little mining town located at the base of the mountains.

"I should have no problem getting help there to find them," the young man thought to himself. "I could get Ike Watson and Matt Prigley, who would gladly go to lend a hand, and there is no better man to take hold of this sort of thing than Ike Watson."

For mile after mile, the horse thieves' tracks remained simple to follow. The trail was so plain to see, the young ranchman soon realized that they had not believed they would be followed. He quickly found himself wrong, however. The tracks suddenly disappeared when he came around a rocky spur of land.

Allen halted in dismay and let out a curse. He looked to the right and the left and ahead, but to no use.

"Here's a pretty state of things," he complained as he gazed around. "Where could their tracks have gone? They couldn't grow wings and fly away."

He dismounted and walked around the edge of the stony ledge for a half-hour, squatting down, trying to spot any clues they might have left. Then on a hunch, he moved forward over the bare rock, feeling pretty certain that it was the only way they could have gone. The barren, rocky way stretched ahead to a gentle dirt slope at the end. Grass grew over it, and bushes dotted it here and there. Several sets of horse tracks marked its surface.

"Hurrah!" he cried, punching his fist into the air. "I see the trail again!"

He hustled back to Lily. He calculated that he had traveled around ten miles so far. His mare showed appearances of being tired, and he spoke to her more kindly than ever.

"Come on, old girl," he said, patting her soft neck. "You can do it. We'll get it all done, and then you can rest for a stretch."

The faithful horse lay back her ears and appeared to understand Allen's every word as he climbed into the saddle. She was a most knowing creature. Allen would have gone wild had she been one of the stolen horses.

"On, Lily," he said, "we'll return Jasper and Rush back before nightfall, or know the reason why."

The horse took off over the plain that stretched before her for several miles, the foothills at last in sight. Beyond them were the mountains, covered with a purplish haze. The mare slowed to a walk as she struck the first upward slope. Hardly had she done so than Allen saw something on the trail ahead that made his heart jump.

A man was riding Chet's horse.

Chapter 2

Chet and Paul watched Allen disappear on the back of his mare up the trail leading to the southwest. Paul shook his head.

"Allen has taken on a dangerous job, this chasing horse thieves. A fellow is apt to get shot, killed maybe, unless he is careful," Paul worried. After a moment, he shrugged and sighed. "But it's no use arguing with Allen once his mind is made up."

"So we let him play a lone hand again," Chet said with a huff. "As always."

"He was right about Lily being tired," Paul pointed out.

"Whose side are you on?" Chet grumbled.

"Allen carries a lot of weight on his shoulders since Pa died," Paul soothed.

"Yes, I know he does," Chet retorted, kicking at the dirt as he always did when upset, "but he doesn't need to haul it around all by himself. We can help if he'd let us."

"You're right," Paul agreed calmly. "We could if he would let us."

Chet kicked at the dirt again. "It's too bad we couldn't go with him. I'd give anything for a good horse now."

"Well, anything you own isn't much at the moment," Paul added, underscoring his words with his quiet sense of humor. "But I agree with you; I wish I had a mount and could go along, too."

"I'm telling you, Paul, if something doesn't turn up right in a couple of hours, I'm going off with my rifle, on foot," proclaimed Chet. "Order or no order. I may not discover anything, but at least trying to do something will ease my mind."

"Perhaps we both ought to stay on the ranch instead," advised Paul. "More unprofitable visitors might pay us a visit."

"I don't think the gang will dare to show up in this vicinity again in a hurry," dismissed Chet. "Like as not,something, they'll steer for Deadwood, sell our horses, and spend their ill-gotten gains at the gambling saloons. That's their usual style. They can't hang around in mountains or on the plains as long as there is money burning a hole in their pockets, no matter whose it was originally. Well, I reckon we can't stand around here all day."

The two boys locked up the barn as well as they could, using a wooden pin they found instead of the broken hasp and padlock. Paul ambled inside the house. Chet went to get the string of fish they had caught in the morning, which they had hastily hung on a bush when they discovered the robbery. Chet fetched them, brought them in, and tossed them into a large tin basin on the table.

"I suppose I might as well fry a couple of these," Chet thought out loud, "though, to tell the truth, I am off my feed."

"I don't have much of an appetite either," said Paul, "but we need to eat, and dinner will help pass away the time. I reckon there is no telling when Allen will be back."

"True."

Chet took the string of fish and chose several of them to clean. He was used to such tasks and did it with a dexterity and quickness that could not have been excelled.

He enjoyed working with his hands. Paul was the reader in the family; he'd be content reading paragraphs on the back of a railway ticket. Chet, though, was happiest when he was busy with his hands, doing anything: making something, building something or repairing something.

While Chet cleaned the fish, Paul checked the shotguns to make sure they were clean and oiled. He loaded them and put them back in their rack. When the fish was finished cooking, Chet set their plates on the table. He set out a third plate automatically, then realized Allen wouldn't be there. He knew Allen wouldn't come back in time to eat, but he decided he might as well leave setting on the table as a little good luck charm.

"That looks delicious as always, Chet," Paul smiled once he sat down.

"You and Allen should be grateful that I took over the cooking duties after Ma died," Chet bragged, dishing out their food. "Everyone else only knew how to open cans of beans."

"You're a great pot rustler!" Paul said.

After Chet took his seat, Paul said grace. Both ate heartily, even though they claimed they were not hungry.

"It's strange," said Chet during the meal. "Allen didn't say anything about his morning trip."

"He was too excited over the theft of the horses to think of anything else, I suppose," Paul replied. "It was enough to upset anyone's mind."

"Perhaps, but at least he might have said if he had any news from Uncle Barnaby," said Chet.

"I imagine if he had heard something he would have said so or left us a letter, if one came, Chet. Allen understands as well as you or I how anxious we really are."

"The way Uncle Barnaby seemed to simply disappear is odd," mused Chet, as he plastered mashed potatoes on his plate with a fork. "One would think a man couldn't go to San Francisco and just vanish off the face of the earth."

Apparently, it was Chet's turn to start today. Like actors in a play, they went through the same dialog, but with the brothers taking different parts. It was as if talking about the strange occurrence over and over and over would somehow change the facts, or illuminate a missed clue, or in some way provide the elusive answer. It never did.

"San Francisco is a big city. He might have been sandbagged or something like that," Paul suggested.

"Oh, you don't actually think such a thing would happen?" Chet always had that thought in mind as a possibility, and was honestly hoping Paul could persuade him differently. He didn't.

"Uncle was," Paul corrected himself, "*is* a great hand to see the sights and also to show off any money he has. Many of the people in that city are a bloodthirsty lot, so I hear."

"Do you really believe his claim of having found a rich gold mine?" Chet asked.

"Well, he discovered something worthwhile. He must have, or he wouldn't travel to Frisco to start a company to develop it."

"We could use the cash now. Especially after..." Chet trailed off in mid-sentence, although they both understood what he referred to.

They continued their meal in silence for a few minutes, the only sounds coming from their forks clinking against the plates. After a second, Chet went on. "They say things come in threes. All we need now is for Captain Grady to show up."

"There's a gloomy thought."

"Well, maybe getting your horse hooked puts you in a gloomy frame of mind," Chet rejoined.

"Pa left matters in a very unsettled condition, unfortunately," Paul said, "and what has become of Uncle Barnaby the world only knows."

"Now who's being gloomy?" chided Chet. "What I'm complaining of is the uncertainty of how things are going to turn out. For all we know, we may be cast adrift, as the saying goes, any day. Grady could throw us off our land."

"Grady will have to fish or cut bait, eventually. He's claimed for years that our title to the ranch is defective, or not good at all. I imagine our claim to the ranch is proper and legal. If those title documents hadn't been burned when one end of the house took fire, I wouldn't worry a bit. Without them, though, Grady still could make a lot of trouble for us."

"I wouldn't be concerned either if we had those, but Captain Grady is the meanest man that ever drew the breath of life, and if he learns that we don't have them, he'll be down on us quicker than a grizzly bear in the spring." Chet stabbed the last of his food with his fork. He continued quietly. "I like it here on the ranch,

Paul. I like to hunt and fish and round up the cattle and the rest ... I don't mind the chores. I don't want to leave."

"Well, we won't let him find out that the papers are destroyed," Paul stated as a simple matter of fact. "We'll continue to fob him off."

"We can't fool him forever. Even Grady. He may just wear us down," Chet said.

"In that case, we'll need to hire an attorney."

"And pay him with what?"

"We'll need to cross that bridge when we get to it," Paul said after a pause.

Chet glanced up at Paul. He was always amazed, and a little jealous, by how unflappable Paul was. Sometimes it was also more than a little irritating. Chet pushed himself away from the table and stood.

"Wash or dry?" he asked as he gathered up the plates and forks.

Paul got up as well. "Dry. You never like how I wash."

Chet grinned as the two moved toward the sink. "For good reason."

Shortly after cleaning up the dishes, Chet and Paul went out to care for the cattle about the place, for quite a few of the herd had already been penned up ready for the early fall drive. The ranch did not boast of many head, and such as there was the brothers desired to keep in the best possible condition so they could receive top dollar. When they had finished their chores, the two leaned on the fence and gazed at their small herd.

"I'm glad they're in the corral," Paul remarked. "I don't want to repeat the other month. Ten hard days of hunting over the long range to find the ones that went astray."

Chet nodded. "We couldn't do that now anyway, with no mounts."

"We're up a tree until he returns with Jasper and Rush," Paul shrugged.

Chet worried about Allen again and thought that the best news would be his safe return with all the horses. Even if he wasn't sure Allen would succeed, he wished to know at least if he would be safe.

Thoughts of the theft and Captain Grady seized Chet again. He needed to do something. He turned to Paul. "We need some more firewood. I'll split the logs and you can stack them."

Chet knew they didn't need anymore, but he also knew that Paul would go along with anything he said to help him. Chet walked over to the shed and grabbed the ax with one hand and assisted Paul with the two-man saw. They went a few yards to where a section of a cottonwood trunk lay on the ground.

The three brothers discovered this downed tree on their property a couple of months ago. Allen decided to drag it back to the ranch instead of cutting it up on the prairie and carting the pieces back a few at a time. Chet thought the idea was dumb, and said so at the time, leading to another argument which required Paul to quell. Bringing the trunk back to the house turned out to be more work than any of them believed, but Allen refused to give up. He treated the whole operation with the seriousness of a general controlling a battle, barking out commands to Chet and Paul. Any obstacle he encountered just seemed to increase his determination to complete the job. Chet finally admitted—to himself—that in the end, Allen's idea was a good one.

Chet and Paul stripped to the waist as they toiled in the hot sun and sawed off a chunk of cottonwood trunk. With skilled hands and a practiced eye, Chet placed one piece of log on the stump, and expertly brought down the ax. It split the wood partway, then Chet worked the blade to divide it into halves. He repeated the action on the smaller pieces. Paul toted the logs to the wood shed, returned to the trunk, and they cut off another section.

As he continued, Chet concentrated on the heft of the ax, the pull of his muscles, the feeling of the warm sun on his bare back, and the rhythm of his chopping, even the sweat running down his torso. Soon, his thoughts turned away from Allen's possible danger.

Paul waited patiently to gather the firewood. When he couldn't fit another stick into the shed, he shuttled it to a growing pile beside the house. Their task absorbed them for over an hour when they heard a cheerful voice hail them. They looked out and saw Ike Watson riding up their trail. He reined up by the brothers.

"Whoop! Hullo there!" greeted the old fellow. He was a big and strong as a bear, and under his long unkempt hair and beard, strongly resembled one. "What's the meanin' of two healthy boys workin' around the ranch on such an all-fired fine day as this?"

"Ike, I'm so glad you happened along!" Chet embedded the ax into the stump and ran to greet him. "We were hoping some friend would come."

"That so?" Ike's face grew sober on the instant. "What's the trouble?"

"Somebody stole our horses!" Chet cried.

"Gee, shoo! Horse thieves again! Well, I'll be eternally blowed!" bellowed Ike, in a rage. "Who be they?"

"We don't know," Paul shrugged. "We think they may be left-overs from the Sol Davids gang."

"Horse thieves is worse than poison," growled Ike. "There ought to be a law to hang every one o' 'em, say I! How many animals did they get?"

"Only the two that were here: Chet's and mine," Paul reported.

"Allen went off after them earlier this afternoon," Chet put in.

"By hisself?" Ike said.

"Yes, I'm afraid so," Paul answered.

"Well, Allen for sure takes after his pa, all righty," Ike said.

"We're worried," said Chet. "We would have gone along, but we haven't a single beast left in the barn."

Ike nodded his shaggy head. "I see. Which way did the varmints go?"

"Allen took the trail over the brook." Paul jerked his head in the direction he took.

"Humph!" Ike scratched his head for a moment. "What's to prevent me goin' after him, boys?"

"Will you?" asked Chet eagerly.

"Certain. I ain't got nuthin' to do, an' if I had, I reckon I could drop it pretty quick to do a favor for my old pardner's orphans," declared Ike. "Why, Granville Winthrup and Ike Watson rode to-gether for years 'til he up and married yer ma."

"Are you well armed?" Paul gestured toward the house. "We have some—"

"Armed? Well, I should say so." Ike produced an old 1849 horse pistol nearly two feet long from his belt. "That is my best friend, barrin' the rifle. Now tell me the particulars."

Paul reviewed the day's events. When he finished, Ike Watson nodded, then started off.

"You'll hear from me before another sun smiles on ye!" he called back over his shoulder. "An' don't ye worry too much in the between time!"

"Thank you, Ike!" the brothers shouted after him. And with a wave, Ike then disappeared down the trail.

"A rather odd fish, truly," chuckled Paul.

"Yes, but with a heart of steel and gold," said Chet. "This state doesn't contain a braver or better hunter than old Ike Watson."

"You speak the truth," Paul said.

"At least I feel more comfortable now that Ike is starting off to hunt up Allen. He'll do everything to help, no matter in what difficulty he might find him. Let's get back to the wood." Chet headed toward the downed tree. He glanced over his shoulder at Paul. "Although I seem to be doing all the work."

Paul crossed his arms and cocked his head to one side. "Says you. To my mind, checking to see if you chop properly is harder than chopping itself. Not only more difficult, but ... also much more entertaining."

Chet understood what Paul was trying to do and was grateful for the diversion. He grinned as he strode up to him and gave his brother a light shove. "What's that? Listen to him! Why, I oughta clean your plow for that remark!"

Paul sneered at Chet. "Are *you* going to clean *my* plow? Ha! Too much mustard!" Paul spat, then pushed up imaginary shirt sleeves. He slapped Chet lightly on the shoulder with the back of his hand. "You have to try it, juniper. Loser washes *and* dries the supper dishes tonight."

"I'll be right there. I'm gonna rip your arm off and beat you over your head with it," Chet taunted. "Then, I'll be nice again!"

The two crouched, arms held wide while they circled each other, throwing insults and increasingly outlandish threats. Chet at last broke the stalemate by charging. The brothers grappled, laughing, each trying to trip the other, with Chet's strength an equal match for Paul's bigger size. They tumbled to the ground, rolling around in the dirt until Paul pinned Chet.

"Brains over brawn!" Paul crowed as he jumped up, fists raised in the air, then he crouched back down into a defensive stance. "I'm looking forward to making a huge mess at supper tonight!"

"How is that any different from any other night?" Chet laughed.

Paul held out his hand and helped Chet to his feet. Chet resumed chopping wood for a few minutes before Paul at last persuaded him that they had plenty. The light of the late afternoon started to fade as they began the round of evening work. They fed the chickens and pigs and made sure that everything was secure for the night. There were also a couple of cows to milk and a dozen or more of eggs to gather.

Chet finished his jobs at his usual express train speed, while Paul worked more methodically. Chet still had some energy to burn and wanted something else to do. He spotted the knot hole in one wall of the tool shed and remembered how much he hated chasing mice out of the small building. Running to the trash pile, he tugged the lid off a can. Holding the jagged edge carefully to avoid cutting himself, he went inside the small building. He placed the round piece of tin over the hole, and secured it with a couple of nails.

"There!" Chet admired his work, "that'll keep the critters out."

He headed toward the house to start dinner. The sun was just beginning to slip behind the mountains. Chet stood in the doorway waiting for Paul. He usually enjoyed watching the slow transition from day into night, but tonight the brilliant red sky reminded him of a wildfire burning his way.

Chapter 3

Allen was hardly mistaken about the horse the man ahead of him rode. He had been on Rush's back many times before and knew the animal's sturdy characteristics. The rider ahead was a stranger to the young rancher, and he did not remember having seen his face before. He intended to see it now, however.

"Stop!" Allen shouted as he urged Lily on. "Stop!"

The stranger caught the words and jerked around in his saddle. He evidently had not known Allen was behind him until then.

"I said stop!" repeated Allen sternly.

"What do you want?" the man shot back over his shoulder. But he did not draw rein an inch.

"Stop, I said," exclaimed Allen, growing more irritated by the second. "That horse belongs to my brother."

"Oh, really?" came the cool reply, but the man did not stop. "Reckon you are mistaken, stranger. This here horse is mine."

"Yours! Your horse? Not much!" sputtered Allen. He had expected the man to either to fight or take to his heels. It was plainly evident that the fellow intended, if possible, to bluff him off. Also equally obvious, he had no intention of stopping on his own. Allen would simply have to do it for him. "Whoa, Rush, old boy!"

The horse halted at the familiar voice and spun around toward Allen. The rider muttered something under his breath as he settled into place on the saddle, gave the reins a vicious yank that made Rush rear up in disgust at the jerk, and said with a scowl to Allen as he rode up, "See here, youngster, keep your parley to yourself!"

"I will—after you get down and turn that horse over to me," Allen said.

"And whyfore should I turn him over to you, seein' as how he belongs to me?" growled the man.

"You stole that horse from our place not four hours ago," he accused. "I'll waste no more words with you. Climb out of that saddle or take the consequences."

"Depend upon it, young fellow, you're a hot-headed youngster, to say the least," came the reply, the man scowling more viciously than ever. He made a movement toward his pistols, but stopped when Allen pulled up his rifle in a rapid motion and took aim.

"I said I would waste no more words with you," Allen said again. "Dismount!"

"Now look here, youngster—"

"Get down!" Allen barked. He cocked his Winchester, causing the man to start back in terror.

"Why, there must be a misunderstanding somewhere, young fella," the man said calmly, and more politely, as soon as he recovered. "My pard turned this critter over to me, and I reckoned it was all right."

"There is where you reckoned wrong," Allen said. "Are you going to get down now or not?"

"Supposin' we talk about it with my pard first?" The man smiled. "Why, there he is now."

The man indicated the trail behind Allen. His manner was so natural that for the instant it deceived the young ranchman. He glanced over his shoulder. The horse thief urged Rush on, digging his spurs deep into the little horse's flesh. He took off in a dash and a clatter.

Allen cursed at his stupidity and grew hot with fury at being so effortlessly duped. Allen aimed his rifle and fired. He missed. The other man dropped partly under the horse's neck to shield himself from another chance shot. Rush was moving along over the rocks too fast for Allen to take the risk of killing his brother's favorite beast. Besides, only a small portion of the rider could be seen at one time.

I'll follow him until a better opportunity presents itself, he thought. He slid the rifle back into its holder and he cried to Lily to pursue.

Once again, his horse responded gallantly. Her ears perked up and her muscles strained. Up and around the bends, she climbed the rocky trail, spurred on by the clattering ahead. The mare struggled to go on, but in less than half a mile she could not go any farther. Her pace slowed and her flanks dripped with sweat. Allen decided not to push her any longer. He dismounted and stroked her neck. "You did your best," he told his horse. "Time to rest." The clattering hooves of their quarry faded away. Allen led his mare off the trail under the shade of a tree. He reached for his canteen and poured the water into his hat, then gave it to Lily to drink from. He returned his hat to his head, its wetness refreshing him in the warm air.

The trail crested the rise about one hundred feet ahead. He crept to the summit, keeping an eye on either side for a possible bushwhacking attack, but all was clear. From this high point, the path descended into a dark pass between two steep hills lined with a few pine trees.

The rider has gone on, that is certain, Allen thought. *I guess he has decided to wear out my horse by riding poor Rush hard.*

Allen wondered what had become of the other thieves and Paul's horse, Jasper. Surely they weren't far away. He figured that the fellow he was following was trying to get to the others, who had probably gone on ahead.

He gazed down the trail, wondering where it led and found himself longing to follow the path, no matter where it ended. He wanted nothing more than to leave his current life behind him and start fresh again, somewhere free of responsibility for others, maybe a place where he could find a sweetheart. Sometimes it seemed as if looking after his brothers and their ranch would wear him down like a boot heel grinding him into little more than a pile of dirt. But as he sat at the bedside that final night, with the fever snuffing out his father's life, he swore a promise. His father lay in a coma, breathing irregularly as his color turned ghastly white. Allen pledged to the wasted figure under the bedclothes that he would watch over his younger brothers always and keep them together. Pa stirred slightly as if he listened and approved. Allen renewed his vow as he stood in tears alone at his father's grave after the funeral service.

He couldn't permit himself to come back empty-handed; he refused not to reach his goal. Chet and Paul depended on him now just as they had for the past two years.

At this moment, though, he needed a course of action. As he thought, he caught something moving out of the corner of his eye. He peered down the trail and saw two riders coming. Allen squinted, and it appeared like the first man was astride Jasper. They hadn't seen him yet. He ran back to Lily and led her behind some rocks.

"Quiet now, Lily," Allen said as he stroked her muzzle, "I need to find out where these two are going."

Allen waited impatiently as the other two plodded up the trail. The closer they got, the more Allen was positive that the man in front was riding Jasper. The man behind rode a mustang and led two others — little animals looking much worn out from constant and hard usage. Apparently he was wrong about who was catching up with whom; these two were going to meet with the first outlaw. As the drew nearer, Allen heard them speak.

"I reckon you've missed the road, Saul," said the man riding behind in a disgusted tone.

"No," came the blunt reply. "I ain't missed nuthin', Darry."

"Well, we don't appear to be makin' much headway," complained Darry.

"Quit yer complainin'," Saul shot back. "We'll come out all right, never fear."

"Well," said Darry, "I move we take a rest anyway."

"I'm tired of ridin' a strange horse over these here hills, too," Saul fired back. "We're meetin' Jeff on the other side of this pass, then we'll sit off and have a bite of the stuff in haversack."

The two rode past Allen and Lily without so much as a glance at them. Allen's plan fell into place: follow these two to their meeting with the first man he encountered riding Rush.

Remaining under the cover of the rocks, he again climbed to the crest of the trail to observe the other riders. They were working their way through the pass. Allen became restless, wondering if they could possibly go any slower. Finally the others reached the bottom of the slope and followed the trail as it turned behind the base of the mountain. When the two men passed out of view, Allen ran back to Lily, and climbed into the saddle.

"On Lily. We must run them down at once."

Allen guided his mount back to the trail and started down the pass. He needed to go fast enough to catch up with the thieves, but not so quickly as to give them a chance to detect him coming up and ambush him.

At the bottom of the slope, Allen dismounted and peered around the rocks. The path ahead was empty and made a detour to the left around a hill covered with cactus and other prickly plants. Allen climbed on his horse again and rode to the next curve. Once again, he slid to the ground and crept around the bend.

The terrain opened up to a broad valley, blanketed with sage and dotted with some trees. About two rods down the trail, the three men sat just off to the side, eating and talking in low tones, while the horses had been tethered to some nearby branches.

Allen had another idea: These men stole his animals, he might as well just steal them back. Allen realized he couldn't just ride up to them; he could never fight two or more among these rocks and bushes in that situation. However, sneaking up and getting a drop on them was possible.

Allen led Lily off the trail, away from the men and hid her again. He drew his revolver and carefully threaded his way between the sagebrush like a puma on the prowl. A couple of times he stopped dead when he stepped on a twig, the snap sounding to him as loud as a thunderclap. Finally, he was near enough to discern words of the men's conversation. He got down to all fours, moving closer until he was within a few feet of Jasper. Watching for a chance, when the backs of the men were turned, Allen holstered his gun, sneaked from his cover and wormed his way toward Paul's horse. He held his breath and wondered why pounding heart didn't burst out of his chest.

When in position, Allen grasped the halter with one hand, holding his knife in another. He noiselessly cut the leather with the blade and then did the same with Rush. The horses whinnied as they recognized Allen, who always made pets of all in the stable. The sound reached the horse thieves and they sprang to their feet. Saul leaped up and ran forward to stop Allen as he started to mount Jasper. He made it to the young man's side just when Allen gained the saddle.

"Come down out of that," Saul cried, roughly grabbing Allen's leg with one hand.

"Not much," scorned the young man. "Out of the way unless you want to get run down."

He urged the horse forward. Jasper started, but before he had taken three steps, Mangle caught him by the bridle. "Whoa!" Saul ordered as he pulled out his revolver. "Whoa, I say!"

"Let go, do you understand?" Allen commanded.

"I won't do it! Darry! Jeff! Come here, why don't you? What are you waitin' for?" Saul angrily yelled.

Allen realized that affairs were turning against him. He leaned forward over Jasper's neck and struck Saul a sharp blow full across his mouth. It came so rapidly that he staggered back and loosened his hold.

"On, Jasper, on, my boy!" Allen slapped the animal's rump with his palm. "Come, Rush! Come, Rush!" he added to Chet's horse, which stood near. Off went Jasper with a bound, and Rush came after his heels.

"Stop him! Hang the measly luck!" roared Saul. "Darry! Jeff! What are you at?"

As he cried out, the leader of the thieves fired his pistol. Allen disappeared behind a clump of cottonwoods as the shot splintered a trunk. The young man was having a hard time of it. He was going it blindly, not knowing where to go next. He realized his peril and clung on desperately, meanwhile urging his mount and his mate to do their best to place distance between them and their pursuers.

Allen pulled out his pistol and fired a shot behind him. He noticed a slopping trail leading down toward a ravine that angled to take him back the way he came. If he got down there, he could double back and pass them out of sight, going in the opposite direction. They wouldn't expect that move.

Another gun shot exploded behind him and the bullet sliced through the air. Allen returned the fire, turned around and headed for the gully. It was a mistake. The slight path he'd been traveling on became rougher and it was difficult to make any progress. Undergrowth and small trees choked the area. The horses were trying their best but were no match on such terrain. Allen urged them forward.

"Halt!"

The first words that greeted Allen's ears were not pleasant ones as he tried to dodge behind some large trees, spotting Saul ahead of him on the higher ground. Saul spoke quickly to his horse, which then leaped towards him, going down in a graceful arc. They landed in a bunch of brush just a few feet away from Allen. Saul fired into the dirt directly in front of Jasper's hooves. The frightened animal jumped up high and pitched Allen, his gun going off in a wild shot as it bounced out of his hand.

"Will you stop fightin' now?" Mangle rode up to fallen rider. Allen climbed to his feet as the other two thieves arrived behind him, guns drawn.

"I knew I told you about that kid, Saul," said one of Allen's captors from behind him to Mangle.

"I thought you said he stopped following you, Jeff," snapped Mangle back at him.

"I said I thought I lost him!" Jeff defended himself weakly. "I thought—"

"That's the trouble when you try to think. It ain't natural for you," said Saul with disgust in his voice.

"I fooled him!" Jeff protested.

"Well, you were wrong about that! Nothing gets me going more than when people take stuff belonging to my brothers!" Allen returned.

"Ah, how sweet. Takin' care of his little brothers. Do you change their diapers, too?" Saul sneered.

Darry and Jeff chortled, repeating "change their diapers" to each other.

Saul thumbed back the hammer up his pistol. "Now, drop the gun belt." Allen did so. "Now, gather those bridles, and walk back to where we started."

Allen took the halters for Jasper and Rush in his hand and walked towards the clearing where the chase began. The others rode their horses, guns trained on him. The only possible thing he could do jumped into his mind. When he reached the remains of the lunch the thieves scattered about when they took off after him, he stopped. Saul stood in front of him. Allen slapped his card on the table.

"Your name is Saul?" Allen asked.

"Saul Mangle," Saul said. "What's it to you?"

"Not a thing but I think I found something you lost."

"Something I lost? What?" Saul's eyes narrowed suspiciously.

"Oh, it isn't anything much really. Only a small silver cross with your initials carved on it. It was about this size." Allen held out one hand with a finger and thumb an inch apart.

"Where did you find it?" the outlaw asked in a tight voice.

"It was found in the barn where you stole those horses," Allen said as he gestured toward Rush and Jasper. "It's enough evidence to send you to the gallows."

"Hand it over," Saul demanded.

Allen took a deep breath. "No."

"Check if he has it on him," Saul said to his companions. Jeff grabbed Allen's arms behind his back and squeezed, while Darry searched through his pockets. He shook his head.

"Idiot, go see if it's around his neck," Saul spat out.

Darry ripped open Allen's shirt and felt around for something under it. "Not here."

"I'll make a deal with you," Allen said. "Let me take back what is rightfully mine, then nobody will ever see or hear of that cross again."

"Where is it?" Saul forced the words out from between clenched teeth.

"I told you my terms," Allen replied. "What is your answer?"

Saul thumbed back the hammer of his pistol and put the barrel of it next to Allen's temple. "I ask again, where is it?"

Allen continued to look straight ahead, trying not to move a muscle aside from regular breathing. "I told you what I want for that cross."

"You don't scare easily, I'll give you that," Saul lowered his gun. He nodded at Darry.

Darry stepped up in front of Allen and punched him in the stomach repeatedly until he could barely breathe.

"Are you ready to tell us?" Saul asked him once Darry stopped.

Allen tried to catch his breath before he answered: "No, you have my deal."

"Keep going," Saul said in a bored voice. The beating continued as Darry worked Allen over in an unrelenting series of body blows. Allen's vision started to blur and shake and his knees buckled. Jeff released him and he slumped to the ground. He curled up in a ball, retching.

Saul kicked Allen in the side as he asked him a question. "You ain't dead yet, are you?"

Allen groaned.

"No?" Saul seemed pleased with the answer. "Good. I'm thinkin' that if I get rid of you, I can cut this tie between me and that cross." He pointed at the prostrate form on the ground. "We know what kind of fella you are." Saul proclaimed to the others, "This hombre looks like a desperate character to me. A common horse thief! We know what the fine, upstandin' citizens of this state do to horse thieves."

Darry answered in fury, "Do what they did to Sol Davids! We should string him up!"

Jeff called out, "We've got to lynch him."

The three men laughed as Darry removed a rope off one of the horses' saddles and began tying it into a noose. He then sat down on the ground like he was settling in for a long job, giggling.

Jeff held Allen up for Saul, who pulled Allen's arms behind his back. Jeff moved aside so that Saul could tie Allen's hands together tightly enough so that he couldn't move them anymore.

After Saul finished his task, they pulled Darry's completed noose down over Allen's head while they adjusted it so it would fit snugly around his neck.

"Use that branch over there," said Saul as he pointed toward one over them on the cottonwood. "This tree is about to start blooming."

The leaves rustled above him as the rope was tossed over the limb. Saul and Jeff lifted Allen on Rush's back, while Darry kept the noose's tension tight.

"Now," Saul instructed, "takes the horse out from under him. Not too fast. I wants him to think about his wicked deeds as he chokes real slow." He tapped two fingers to his hat brim in a mocking salute. "See you in hell, youngster."

Jeff took Rush's halter and began to lead him forward. Allen suddenly became peaceful and, strangely, accepting. His eyes closed, and he was already thinking about Paul and Chet when they heard of his death. A carousel of thoughts churned in Allen's head. He felt his stomach sink as he slipped off Rush's back. He swung free in the air.

Chapter 4

Morning found Paul tired, groggy, and cranky. The night had been long to the two boys, neither of whom had slept more than an hour at a time, both tossing and turning. Paul alerted to every noise, trying to shape whatever the sound was into an approaching horse, although he knew Allen wouldn't travel on a moonless night.

At daybreak, Paul listened to Chet dress, rush out of the room they shared and climb up on the roof of the ranch house. About ten minutes later, Chet returned, holding their father's field glasses.

"Not a man or horse in sight," sighed Chet in deep disappointment, hanging the binoculars over a bedpost.

"Allen hasn't been gone twenty-four hours yet," Paul reminded him.

"But Ike said we'd hear from him before morning!" Chet complained.

"Ike is doing his best, I'm positive. The chase may be a long one." Paul tried to sound reassuring as he sat up in his bed, although he didn't feel it. "Most likely they stopped in somewhere to spend the night, but Allen ought to be back by noon. He knows we will be eager to hear how he made out."

"I hope you're right," Chet grumbled as he left the room.

Paul groaned as he climbed out of bed and pulled on his trousers. Picking up the pitcher from the washstand, he stepped into the main room.

The house's largest room served multiple needs: living, dining, and an office. Directly across from the two brothers' bedroom was the front door, flanked by two windows. Under the left one stood a settee, the one concession to comfort in the place; an item their mother insisted on, Paul remembered with a warm smile.

The round dining table sat in the center of the room, circled by five straight-back chairs. A large, roll-top desk and swivel chair took up the wall between the room occupied by Paul and Chet and the one used by Allen. A door in the left wall formerly led to a storage room, which burned down last year. The brothers salvaged enough wood to fashion a small closet in its place, and they also added a small window to the right of the door. The gun rack hung to the left of the door. A stone fireplace, with the sixth straight-back chair next to the hearth, made up the right-hand wall, as well as the open arch to the small, lean-to kitchen. Paul's small, prized library, made up of dog-eared books and old magazines on any and all subjects he managed to scrounge up over the years, rested to the right of the fireplace in a short bookcase he built.

Paul padded into the kitchen, added some water Chet always had heating on the stove to the jug, and returned to the washstand. He poured some water in the bowl and began to wash his face. The sounds of a horse's hoofs broke upon his ears.

"Is that Allen, Chet?" Paul called out, but then his face fell. "No, it's not his style of riding."

Chet burst into the room.

"Captain Grady!" the youngest brother announced, pointing behind him. "He's on his way up the trail!"

Paul leaned on the washstand's marble top and let out an irritated breath. "Great. Wonderful. Just the last person I wanted to see this morning. Or ever, truth be told."

"Why do you think he's coming here?" Chet asked anxiously.

Paul shook his head. "I'm sure I don't know."

"Perhaps he found out the papers are burned," Chet suggested with some alarm.

"I doubt he learned the title is destroyed. None of us told him, and there is no other way he could find out," Paul said.

"Maybe he's got more evidence to prove he owns the place," Chet said. "Troubles never come singly, true enough! I told you they came in threes."

Paul pushed himself up from the washstand. Chet stood on the threshold, like a soldier waiting for an order.

"Go greet our welcome guest. I'll be out presently." Paul spoke in an acid-dripping voice as he waved a hand toward the porch. He recalled Chet's tendency to interrupt conversations. "Remember, let me do the talking."

Chet nodded, then darted from the room as Paul grabbed the piece of coarse linen off the rod at the end of the washstand and dried his face. He angrily wadded up the material and stuffed it back over the rack. He stopped.

No, don't lose your temper, he told himself. *Keep your emotions under control. Use your brains. Outsmart him.*

"That won't be too difficult with Grady," Paul mumbled to himself.

Paul took a deep breath, retrieved the crash, folded and neatly replaced it. He snatched his shirt off his bed. A small smile stole across his face, then he tossed the garment back down. He picked up the bowl of soapy water and headed for the porch.

Chet left the front door open. Paul steeled himself before walking outside to meet the new arrival. He stopped next to his brother on the porch. Captain Hank Grady sat on his horse a few feet away, as if poising for a statue.

Captain Grady was a tall, hatchet-face man of forty or so years of age. He possessed the sour disposition of one assured in his own superiority, but annoyed the rest of the world had not yet acknowledged that obvious fact.

"Good morning." Paul greeted him with all the pleasantness he could muster. "What brings you out here this fine morning?"

"Hullo, there, young fellers," Grady called out, his attempt at sounding friendly coming off as natural as a snake square dancing. He dismounted. "I reckon you didn't expect to see me quite so soon again, did you?"

"We did not. That is correct," rejoined Paul, coolly.

Paul waited until Grady walked a few steps closer to the porch, then he casually emptied the contents of the bowl in the general direction of Grady's feet. He enjoyed watching the unwanted visitor hop backwards to avoid getting splashed.

"Well, I confess I fixed matters up quicker than I first calculated to do," the captain went on, glaring at Paul. "I thought I was going to have a good bit more trouble to establish my claim."

"As far as we know you have none here to make," said Paul. "You may pretend—"

"Listen here, I ain't goin' to talk to you," retorted Captain Grady, cutting him short. "Your big brother is the feller I want to see—him or Barnaby Winthrup."

"Both of them are away," Paul replied politely, although his irritation was rising at the newcomer's aggressive behavior. He tamped down the sparks of anger before they could burst into flame.

"Paul and I are running the ranch just now!" Chet put in.

"So we are the only ones here you can talk with at present. If you don't like my manner of speech you need not stay," Paul said.

"Ho! Don't you dare speak that way to me, you young half-naked savage!" roared Captain Grady. "I didn't come here to deal with a couple of kids."

"We may be young, but we have rights here, just the same," challenged Chet.

"My brother is correct," noted Paul. "If you wish to talk business, you must do so with both of us, or wait for the others to return."

Grady glowered in silence for a few seconds.

"All right, all right, I'll go over this concern with you youngsters," Captain Grady spat out. He tied his horse fast to a porch post and strode into the house.

"Please do come in," Paul mumbled as Captain Grady brushed past him.

Paul glanced at Chet, shrugged and followed inside. Captain Grady was looking around the place as if measuring for new drapes. He started to wander toward the open desk. Paul maneuvered around the table in the opposite way to block Grady's path. Putting the bowl on the table, he rolled the desktop closed.

"I'm sorry I ain't got your older brother to palaver with," began the captain, looking a little irked that Paul outflanked his move. "I reckon he is the one who will understand my talk best."

"Then, perhaps you should call again when he gets back," proposed Paul pleasantly.

"And when will that be?" Captain Grady asked.

"I really cannot say exactly." Paul smiled and gestured toward the open door.

"Well, I'm not in the humor to wait. It's been too long already." The captain paused and cleared his throat pompously. "I believe you said you had the title papers for this property, didn't you?"

"Yes, we did say that," Paul agreed.

"I would like to look at 'em." Captain Grady's request was not polite.

Chet and Paul exchanged worried glances. They had expected and dreaded this moment. Paul unnecessarily shifted the empty bowl on the table, taking a little longer than needed to let him think about his next move.

"Supposing we don't care to show them to you?" said Paul.

"What's the reason you don't care to?" demanded the captain.

"We are not called on to explain all our actions to you," yelled Chet. He ran up next to his brother.

Paul squeezed Chet's shoulder with one hand as a reminder to keep quiet.

"Look here, I don't want to quarrel, but I'm a-goin' to see them there papers," blustered Captain Grady, with a decided shake of his head. "I came all the way from town to look at 'em."

"Then I'm afraid you traveled out here for nothing. You won't see them," Paul said.

"Well, in that case, I reckon I'm free to speak what's on my mind," bellowed the captain, "an' that is, that you never had no papers at all."

"You can say what you please." Paul spoke as calmly as he could.

"An' that ain't all I'm gonna to say," the captain plowed on. "I got more to say to you. This here claim o' land originally belonged to Sam Slater, o' Deadwood—"

"We know that," Paul acknowledged.

"Slater died, with no will—"

Paul nodded. "That may all be true, too."

"An' he left this land—"

"No, he didn't. My father bought the ranch from Mister Slater before died," Paul corrected.

"No such thing. This property is part o' Old Slater's estate, and he sold it to me."

"He did not."

"He did too! An' I can take my affidavy, if one is necessary," exclaimed Captain Grady with growing irritation. "But that ain't all yet I got to tell. Slater willed the property to his heirs, an' I bought it from them only last week."

"That can't be true!" gasped Chet, faintly.

"It is, an' I have the papers to prove it," said Captain Grady. "This here ranch belongs to me, an' the sooner you boys pack up your things an' get out, the better it will please me."

Captain Grady planted his fists on his hips and smiled at the boys in malicious triumph.

Both Paul and Chet stared at the speaker as if they had not heard right. Paul found his voice first.

"You say you bought the ranch and possess the documents to prove your ownership?" he clarified.

"What are you, deaf? I just said that, boy."

"Your claim will not hold water," Paul declared simply.

"Well, I reckon it will," rebuked Captain Grady. "I allow as how I know what I'm a-doin'."

"My father bought this ranch, legally, and passed it down to all three of us when he died, in a legal will. In our minds, and in the eyes of the law, that settles the matter. We will not give up our rights here just on what you say." Paul crossed his arms across his chest. "Perhaps we had better take a look at your documents."

"Supposing I don't care to show 'em to you?" sneered Captain Grady. "I got 'em and that's enough. I ain't got to show my papers no more than you got to show yours."

Paul racked his brain what to say next, then something he picked up reading one of his magazines popped into mind. He almost smiled, but rapidly suppressed it.

"I read once that possession is nine points of the law," Paul said, "and we are currently in possession. You cannot take this ranch unless you start a lawsuit to recover this property."

"I ain't a-goin' to wait for no jumped-up circuit judge—" Captain Grady began.

"You seem to have a dread of the law," Paul observed. "Why is that, if your claim to this land is fair and square, as you say?"

"I said I ain't a-goin' to dilly-dally on the law, or for your Uncle Barnaby or for your brother to return, for that matter," went on Captain Grady. He made a sweeping gesture encompassing the entire house. "I want you to leave at once, bag and baggage. Do you understand? Get out!"

"I'm curious. What makes you so desirous for this ranch?" asked Paul. "It's not as grand as your place. You appear to be awfully anxious—"

"Why I want it is my business," growled the captain.

"Do you believe there's wealth concealed on the land?" Paul questioned.

"No, there ain't," Captain Grady fired back, almost so fast that it did not sound natural.

"Because you should know my father and Uncle Barnaby went over every foot of the ground half a dozen times and found nothing. They're both better prospectors than you," Paul said.

"I own the next spread over, that's why I want this one. I want to turn my cattle an' such in the two. Besides that, it ain't natural for a man to stand by an' see others a-usin' of his things."

"Your things? You talk very positively," said Paul. "You can do that all you want, but it will do you no good. We shall not budge at this time."

"You won't?" Captain Grady looked as though he was going to burst a blood vessel.

"Not a step," Paul asserted. "We claim this property and you will need to get the law to throw us out if we are to be put out at all."

"You young highflyers!" blasted out the captain. "Do you think I'll stand such talk?"

"You'll just have to," taunted Chet. "We won't move an inch until the sheriff or a constable puts us out."

For the moment Captain Grady was speechless. His face grew dark with gathering wrath, and he looked as if he wanted to eat someone up.

"So you won't leave, hey?" he hollered at last.

"No," Paul and Chet said together.

"What are you, deaf?" Paul pitched in.

"I'll put you out!" Captain Grady jabbed his finger at the boys.

"I don't think you will," answered Paul.

"Not without a big fight," added Chet.

Grady turned to leave.

"By the way, where did you obtain the title of captain?" inquired Paul as he leaned back against the table. "Nobody seems to know. Did you serve in the army or navy during the war? Or is it some kind of self-bestowed honor?"

Captain Grady stared at Paul with venomous hatred, then snorted out a breath like an angry bull. Without another word, he turned on his heel, and stalked out of the house. He sprang on his horse and rode away at top speed.

"Phew! But isn't he mad!" laughed Chet, as the rider disappeared up the river trail. "But he can stay put out as long as he pleases. He can't stampede over us."

"You bet!" responded Paul. "I don't think he is so sure of his position as he pretends to be. If he knew all was right with his claim, he wouldn't bluster so much and wouldn't be shy about going to the law."

"That's my idea of it, too," Chet said. "I don't believe he ever bought the land. It was probably sold to Uncle Barnaby first."

"Well, 'Captain' Grady is a fool," said Paul, dismissing the visit, "but a fool who doesn't realize he's one can be a danger."

He picked up the bowl and started for the brothers' room.

"Paul?"

He stopped and turned around. "Yes?"

"Paul ... what if ... what if Allen doesn't come back?" Chet asked in a small voice.

A lump rose in Paul's throat, and he swallowed it. "Don't say things like that, Chet. Don't even think it."

"You've had the same thought, I'm sure," Chet pressed. "You said yesterday it was dangerous what he did, going after horse thieves. A fellow is apt to get shot, maybe killed dead, if he is not careful. You said so. What will we do if he doesn't come back? You're smart ... the smartest of us three. Even Allen says so. What would we do?"

Paul hesitated. "Well, I suppose we have to cross—"

"Don't say 'we'll have to cross that bridge when we get it'! You always say that, and it doesn't help!" Chet shouted. He stomped out of the house, slamming the door behind him.

Paul knew what he said ducked the question; it wasn't even an answer in the first place. He carried the bowl back to their room and set it on the washstand. With a sigh, he dropped down to his bed.

What would they do if Allen didn't return? Chet was correct; that awful thought had entered Paul's mind repeatedly during the previous sleepless night and refused to be put out in the cold. Thinking about it tore up his insides, once pushing him to the brink of tears.

The problem was he couldn't logically come up with a clear solution, or even a set of actions to take, and that just increased his upset. He had no idea how to address the question.

Grady's threats added more weight. Paul won the skirmish today, but what about tomorrow, or the next day, or the day after that? The captain certainly had turned into an implacable foe. He would be back.

"We'll have to cross that bridge when we get to it," Paul said to himself.

It didn't help.

He stood, finished dressing and went outdoors to start his chores.

Chapter 5

The outlaws jeered at Allen as the pressure increased inside his head. He felt as if his eyeballs were going to burst through their sockets. His tongue escaped his clenched teeth.

The world grew darker and strange flashes of light pulsed before him. Loud pops reverberated through his skull, then a louder pop seemed to come from the outside. The voices of the bad guys stopped. A second shot sounded in the distance. The ground rose up and smacked him. The noose loosened; he concentrated on sucking in the sweet air as a familiar voice boomed through the darkness.

"Saul Mangle, as I'm a natural born sinner, and Darry Nodley and Jeff Jones! Well! Well! Well! Turn about, before it's too late, ye serpents!"

"Ike?" Allan said with a cracked voice. "Is that you?"

The blackness retreated from Allen's vision, and the returning light made him squint. He watched as the dark mass retreated, exposed by the brightening light. Ike Watson sat astride his horse, rifle at the ready. Allen's vision cleared, revealing Ike as a dark silhouette against the lightening sky.

"The jig's up for the present," grumbled Nodley.

"Raise yer right hands, pick out yer guns with two fingers of yer left hands. Toss yer irons in front of my friend," Ike commanded.

The bandits did so, glowering all the while.

"Have them leave the haversack," Allen put in.

"Ye heard him!" Ike called out. Jeff took the bag off one of the mustangs, and tossed it to the ground.

"Clear out, do ye hear me?" ordered Ike Watson to the crowd of three. "Don't wait for me to git more riled up."

"Come on, we had better vamoose!!" whispered Saul Mangle, with a scowl, and the trio of thieves jumped on their mounts. They disappeared down a side trail, Ike following. There was the sound of more gunfire and Ike bellowing "faster! Let me see yer horse's hoofs!" A few minutes later, Ike rode back, chuckling.

"By the grasshoppers of Kansas, what ye been up to, Allen!" exclaimed old Ike as he sprang down.

"I'm eternally grateful you happened by, Ike," the young ranch-man said.

"Gee shoo, Allen! I didn't jest happen along. I was at your place earlier, and Paul and Chet tell me about the horse thievery. They was worried about ye." Ike removed the noose and tossed it into the bushes with a disgusted look. "For mighty good reason, it seems. So I tracked you."

Allen got to his feet awkwardly with Ike's help. "But those villains—"

"Gone, boy, gone." Ike untied Allen's hands. "They knowed better not to stay where Ike Watson was, ho! Ho!"

"They're outlaws," declared Allen as he rubbed his wrists, "and should be locked up."

"That Saul Mangle ought to be strung up, ye mean," Ike retorted, "and Darry Nodley and that Jeff Jones, they ain't much better. But they're gone now. Why the haversack?"

"They also took our savings. I'm hoping ..." Allen rushed to the bag and searched its contents. His face fell as he threw the sack to the ground. "Our money is not in here. They must have given the loot somebody else, or maybe buried it somewhere. Well, I have Paul's and Chet's horses, at least," added Allen with satisfaction. "Now let me retrieve Lily and we'll head back."

"Whoa, there Allen!" Ike held up his hands. "The hour is gettin' late, and we'll lose the sun. No moon tonight."

"But I need to get back," Allen protested. "Chet and Paul—"

"I telled Paul and Chet I'd be back in the morning," Ike said.

"But they—"

"They be old enough to take look after themselves," said Ike. "Ye needn't worry too much on their account. 'Sides, the horses need a rest."

It was obvious that Ike had made up his mind they were staying here for the night, no matter what Allen thought. He opened his mouth to protest, then didn't.

Arguing with the man who saved your life was ungrateful.

***

It was early afternoon when Paul paused his chore in the vegetable garden. He pulled up a carrot, knocked off the dirt, and started munching on it as he leaned on the hoe. He worked for a short time longer when the sound of hoof beats reached him. Dropping the tool, he loped over to the fence and leaned on the top rail. The crisp sounds of horseshoes striking the hard-packed earth carried through the air. A huge grin broke out on his face. A pair of riders came trotting up the trail, leading two other horses.

"Chet!" Paul called out. "It's Allen and Ike! They're back! They have Jasper and Rush, too!"

Chet appeared by his side almost immediately. The two excitedly ran to the front of the house and waved as they waited for Allen and Ike to ride up. After what seemed to Paul an eternity, the group reached them.

The reunion was chaotic. Shouting out thanks to Allen and Ike, Paul and Chet rushed to their horses. Jasper and Rush nickered when they saw their owners, nuzzling them back. Ike's raucous laughter blanketed the entire scene.

"Ike, how can we thank you?" shouted Chet. He giggled as Rush licked his cheek.

"Well, I'm hungry 'nough to eat a saddle blanket," Ike hinted with a wink.

"I catch your idea!" cried Chet. "You and Allen come in for the biggest, bestest meal ever!"

Ike climbed off his mount. "That sure sounds good!"

Paul took Rush's reins. "I'll take Rush and Ike's horse."

"Thank you, Paul!"

Chet and Ike went into the house, Ike's arm around Chet's shoulders. Paul had to laugh at the size difference between the two. He transferred Rush's bridle to the same hand as he held Jasper's, and held out his other hand.

"Here, let me take Lily, too," he said.

"No, I'll do it." Allen slid off his mount.

"Of course." Paul smiled. He and Chet always joked that Lily was Allen's "favorite gal" since he rarely allowed anybody else to care for her.

Paul took the reins of Ike's horse in his free hand and started walking the three beasts toward the barn. Allen was next to him, leading Lily. They didn't say anything for a few moments.

"Captain Grady came by this morning," Paul said.

"What does he want now?" Allen's voice was weary.

"The same as always," Paul responded. "Now he claims he bought the land from one of Mister Slater's heirs before Pa did."

Allen let out an oath. "We won't stir. Let him sue Uncle Barnaby, if he can. We have nothing to do with it. Our first duty is to find our uncle."

"Of course it is. But what are we going to do if he does, Allen? Or if he tries to evict us?" Paul pressed.

Allen shook his head. "I can't think about it now."

"Perhaps we need to go into Deadwood and get a lawyer—" Paul began.

"Not now, Paul," Allen cut him off curtly.

"Sorry."

Paul and Allen entered the barn. Allen loosened Lily's saddle, while Paul removed Jasper's. They both hoisted their saddles on the rack at the same time. Allen's shirt was open, and Paul noticed the red marks around his neck with some concern.

"What happened out there, Allen?" Paul asked as he went to Rush and loosened the saddle.

"Nothing much," Allen answered as he pulled off Lily's blanket. "Ike and I sneaked up on the thieves, chased them away and took Jasper and Rush back."

Paul set the saddle on a rack next to Jasper's. Allen led Lily into her stall, and Paul moved to Rush. The two worked together silently for a few minutes.

"What happened out there, Allen?" Paul repeated.

"You already asked that." His brother began to brush Lily.

"You didn't answer yet." Paul faced Allen. He tapped his neck in the same spot where the burns were on Allen's neck.

Allen's hands instantly flew up to his collar and tightened it. The two boys stared at each other for a few seconds, Allen's eyes hard. At last, he spoke.

"The thieves caught me trying to free Jasper and Rush," he reported in a taut voice. "They put a rope around my neck and strung me up before Ike arrived."

"Allen!" Paul gasped.

Allen dismissed the occurrence with a shake of his head and a shrug. He resumed rubbing down his mare. "There was nothing to it. I walked away all right. There was no harm done."

"You were almost murdered!"

"Well, I wasn't. Almost doesn't count," Allen said. "I asked Ike not to tell you or Chet about it."

"Why?" Paul demanded.

"Because I didn't think you two needed to know," Allen flung back.

"What were you afraid of? Our reaction? That we couldn't take it? Stop being such a mother hen! Chet and I aren't children!" Paul challenged.

Allen turned back to Paul and jabbed a finger in his direction. "That's for me to decide. You know now what happened. You are not to tell Chet."

Paul sputtered angrily.

"Do not tell Chet," Allen emphasized, his eyes blazing.

"Is that an order?" Paul fired back.

"Yes."

Paul snapped off a sarcastic salute. "Aye-aye, sir."

The two went on stabling the horses in a tense quiet. Allen finished with Lily and patted her on the back. He headed for the barn door. "You coming?"

Paul shook his head. It required an effort to keep his voice steady. "Almost done. Just a few minutes longer."

Allen walked out of the open doors, and Paul followed a couple of quick footsteps. He wanted to race after Allen and punch him in the jaw for how he spoke about him and Chet. He was furious with his brother. *He* would decide when they weren't children anymore! They weren't children now! Of all the …

The middle brother spun around, seething, and gripped a side of one stall, his knuckles turning white. Paul didn't like strong emotions. He didn't want to be mastered by them; he didn't want anything to interfere with his cherished thought and logic. He stuffed down the feelings boiling up in him, forcing the lid shut, until he regained control. Taking a deep breath, he completed his work with Jasper and Rush and he went to the house.

Chet and Ike's laughter greeted Paul as he crossed the porch and went inside the welcoming, cool interior of the house. Ike sat at the table, his plate loaded with food as Chet dished out even more potatoes. Allen stood by himself, staring out the window, coffee cup in hand.

"No, worse luck, they didn't," Ike was saying. "So here's a comin' straight over the mountain was all these buffalo. A huge herd of 'em. They came around on both sides, an' before I knowed it, I was smack-dab right in the center o' 'em."

"What did you do?" asked Chet, wide-eyed as he held his spoon in midair.

"At first I didn't know what to do persackly. Then of a sudden my horse got afeared and shot me over his head into a big thorn bush and made off like a streak o' greased lightnin', leaving me alone," Ike went on.

"With the buffalo all around you?" Chet sat, not taking his eyes of Ike.

"Jest so, more'n twenty o' 'em, and more'n a hundred others comin' up fast as they could leg it. I kin tell ye I was in a fix an' no error."

"The thorns must have hurt plenty," Chet said.

"Hurt?" Ike poked his fork toward Chet. "Well say, it was like bein' dumped into a pit full o' daggers, that was! Tain't forget the awful stickin' pain an' never will! But bein' chucked into that thorn bush saved my life."

"Didn't the buffalo touch the bush?" Chet asked.

"Nary a one," went on Ike. "They would come up close, on a dead run, an' then shy like skittish horses afore a bit o' white paper. Time an' again I thought one would heave hisself atop o' me an' squash me, but the time didn't come. Say, but it was a sight, that was! Them buffalo was mad, clean stark mad, and trampled all over each other. The stampede didn't last more than three minutes."

"Why, Ike," Paul commented with a broad grin as he took his place at the table, "I thought you walked tippy-toe over the backs of the buffalo to get away."

Ike roared with laughter and slapped the table with a massive hand. All the dishes and utensils jumped. "That 'twas the other time!"

"Paul, Paul! Wait until you hear about Allen and Ike and the horse thieves!" Chet yelled out as he placed a dish groaning with food in front of Paul. "Go on, Ike, tell Paul! Tell him everything, and don't you dare leave anything out!"

Paul looked toward Allen. Allen continued to stare out the window, unaffected by Chet's comment. Paul thought strong sunlight streaming in made Allen look years older.

Ike launched into the tallest of tall tales, embellishing the story with wildest, most improbable elements possible, until both Paul and Chet were laughing helplessly.

After Ike polished off two heaping plates of Chet's cooking, he left to a chorus of "goodbyes" and "thank yous." Chet accompanied Ike to the barn, carrying some wrapped leftovers.

"Ike and his taradiddles! They never get old! I certainly enjoyed them," Paul chuckled as he mopped the last bit of gravy with a chunk of bread, "I haven't laughed that hard for a long time. Boy, it sure felt good." He cast a glance at Allen, still standing at the window. "You didn't have any food. Chet outdid himself."

"I didn't want anything," Allen replied tonelessly.

There was an awkward pause.

"I guess you didn't find our savings," Paul ventured.

Allen shook his head. "They didn't have it with them."

"Oh. Too bad."

"Chet's gone into the barn." Allen turned to Paul. "Now tell me about Grady."

"A lot has happened to you, Allen. Grady can keep until morning. We can't do anything about it today anyway," Paul said gently. "Get some rest. You need it."

"Do I need to repeat myself?" Allen asked sharply.

"No, Allen, no you don't," sighed Paul. He told about the captain's morning visit.

When Paul finished explaining, Allen put his mug on the table with a loud clunk and slowly walked to the desk. He sprawled in the chair and then he rubbed his eyes. After a long moment, he breathed a deep sigh and his hands fell to his lap.

"We're going to have to be on the lookout for Grady." Allen stared at the floor. "He is no longer just a mere annoyance."

"I reckon not," Paul returned, "but I don't believe he has any papers—I mean, legal ones. Nothing that would stand in a court."

"No, that dog won't hunt, all right," Allen said, "but he could try other things."

"Such as?" Paul's voice held a note of worry.

"Running his cattle on our spread, like he threatened," Allen went on. "Maybe even trying to fence off the water. One of us should patrol our range every day to keep an eye on him."

"All right. I'll go first, tomorrow morning," Paul volunteered. "I'll stay out a few days."

Allen nodded and pushed himself out of the chair. He did not look like a seventeen-year-old; instead, he looked like a seventy-year-old. Without saying anything else, he walked into his room and closed the door behind him.

Chapter 6

The next morning, Paul packed Jasper with his bedroll and food and set out for a few days of glorious solitude. Their acreage was fairly sizable; it ran up and down the river for nearly a mile, at the edge of the foothills, and stretched up the side of the second dip in the foothills. Paul traveled leisurely around the brothers' land, encountering nothing unusual. In the late afternoon, he stopped at one of his favorite spots that overlooked a deep ravine. It was all there: the water moving quickly through the canyon, the mountains, the glorious blue sky. He breathed deeply.

Paul basked in the warmth of the sun for a moment, then dismounted. He led Jasper to a patch of grass under some nearby trees to graze and strolled back to the very lip of the rimrock to drink in the vista. A deep growl whirled him around.

A large brown and gray grizzly weighing at least seven hundred pounds stood on a nearby outcropping of rocks. Even though their spread's name was the "Big Bear Ranch," this was only the second one Paul had seen since they had lived in that section. He couldn't help but gaze in awe at the impressive and beautiful creature.

Hardly any time had passed when there was another roar. Then a heavy weight filled the air, and the bear leaped down on the ground between Paul and his horse. Jasper whinnied and backed away. The grizzly half turned to face him, then reared up on its hind legs to its full height of eight feet. Paul's breath caught in his throat; he stared up at how powerful it was. The animal looked between Paul and Jasper, almost as if deciding which one to pursue.

Paul hoped he wouldn't need to shoot the magnificent beast, but wished he had his Winchester from his saddle holster. He reached for his Bowie knife, snapped into its holder on his belt. That wouldn't be much help against this gigantic creature, so he drew and cocked his pistol. He waited for the bear to make its next move.

Ike said many times that grizzlies were tough and could stand many shots, as long as they did not hit their vital parts. Paul couldn't waste bullets. If the animal did come after him, Paul would have to hold his fire as long as he could to permit him to take aim. He took a deep breath and prepared himself as much as he could.

The grizzly dropped back to all fours and stared at Paul intently. Rocking side to side, the bear lowered its head, laid back its ears, and huffed a few times. Then it charged Paul.

Overcome with fear, Paul raised his weapon and instinctively stepped back, but his foot snagged on a rock and he stumbled. His revolver discharged harmlessly into the air and then it flew out of his hand. He tottered on the edge of the cliff and flapped his arms like a bird trying to take off, but it didn't work. He pitched over the side of the gorge.

Paul plunged out of the sunlight into the gloom and mist. Only a few seconds passed and with a resounding splash, he made contact with water. Down, down, down he sank, reaching the bottom of the river. The swiftly flowing current caught him in its grasp, tumbled him over and over and sent him spinning downstream. Paul lost consciousness. How long he stayed that way he didn't know. When he came to, he found himself lying among the brush, partly in and out of the water. He attempted to sit up and in doing so slipped off the bank into deeper water. But the instinct of self-preservation remained with him, and he made a frenzied clutch at the bushes and struggled to pull himself out of the torrent up onto a slice of land.

He lay still for several minutes, exhausted. His brain wasn't working, for his head felt as if it was swimming around in a balloon.

At last, he began to come to himself and after a bit sat up to gaze about him, but it was dark and little or nothing was clearly visible. Paul waited nearly half an hour before he felt strong enough to get to his feet. His head was light, and for a while he staggered like a drunken man.

He realized he was a long way from the top. He struggled to keep his emotions at bay, knowing that he would need to rely on his logic and reasoning to escape.

"I can't climb up in this darkness," he said to himself. "I might slip and break my neck. I had better walk some more and search for some natural upward slope."

Now that he had his plan, he started off along the river side, the top of the canyon towering almost a hundred feet above his head as he proceeded. The opening gradually grew narrower, and with this the distance between the rocks and the water decreased, until barely enough room allowed Paul to walk.

"I must have made a mistake," he groaned out loud. "I should have gone up the river instead of down. The chances are that I can't go over a hundred feet farther, if that."

He was right. Soon Paul came to a halt, the ground between the wall of the canyon and the water ending just before him. Beyond that, the steep and bare rocks ran immediately downward into the stream.

"Damn, that settles it," he muttered, in great disappointment. "All this traveling for nothing. And it's night overhead!"

Paul paused to rest for a while, for in his weak condition the walk tired him. After a while, he started to retrace his steps. He had only taken a yard's advance when his left foot slipped on a round stone. Paul pitched over on his side, and before he could save himself, he plunged headfirst into the river again.

He desperately tried to regain the bank, but to no use. The current of the water grew extra strong at this point—the width of the course having shrunk to a mere few dozen yards' space—and before he could clutch a branch or rock or root, the churning water swept him off his feet and towards the other side, where nothing but steep, slippery rocks lined the way back to shore. Vainly he put out his hands to stop his movement, frantically grabbing by every means in his power to obtain some sort of hold somewhere. The sky grew blacker as the walls on both sides began to blur over his head.

He almost cried out for help, and took a breath to do so, but the sound did not come. What would be the use? Not a soul would hear him.

Paul refused to give in to the despair that threatened to take hold. On and on he went, until the water grew colder by the instant, even as his outlook became grimmer.

Although he was a strong swimmer, the roaring current attempting to suck him into the depths. He had never explored this stream fully, and he knew that this situation could not end well for him.

If this ends in some sort of sink-hole, I'm a goner sure, he thought. *But I never heard of one up here among the mountains, so I won't give up just yet.*

The thought had just occupied his mind when, on looking up, he saw the last trace of evening fade from sight. The river had entered a cavern, and the water had now taken him underground.

All was black around and overhead; beneath flowed the dark and cold water, and the only sound that fell upon his ears was the rushing along of the stream.

As well as he could, Paul put out his hands before him, to ward off the shock of a sudden contact of any sort, for he did not know but that he might be dashed to pieces on a jagged rock at any instant.

On and on he went, the torrent several times making turns, twisting first to one side and then to the other. Once his hand came brushing up to a series of rocks, but before he could grasp them the current hurled him farther in an awful blackness. The river seemed to enjoy toying with him like a cat does to a mouse.

Perhaps a quarter of an hour went by. This time stretched like an eternityupward, to Paul. He guessed that he covered a mile or more. The water, however, appeared to slow down, and he suddenly began to feel as if he were standing in a larger space.

This must be an underground lake, he decided. *Now if I—Ah, bottom!*

His thought came to a sudden termination, for a couple of feet below the surface of the stream, his feet had touched a sloping rock. It angled up to his right and moving in that direction, so Paul, to his relief, dragged himself out of the water and on a stony shore.

He sprawled on the ground, catching his breath, a miserable, soggy thing. He was truly high although not dry, at least. This fact was a cheering one, but there was still a dismal enough outlook. Where was he and how would he ever be able to gain the outer world once more?

Despair threatened to drown him as surely as the river tried. Paul clenched one fist and slammed it against the rocks.

"No," he said to himself, "God would not have saved me from the fall and the water, just to let me die in here. That is not logical. So, therefore, there must be a way out. I have to find it."

Keeping the sound of the stream behind him, Paul crawled away for a few yards, as helpless as a blind baby. He slowly climbed to his feet, one hand held above his head in case the cave's roof wasn't very high. He stood all the way up without coming in contact with any rock. He was too exhausted to do more than move about carefully, so he took several cautious steps in many directions, arms outstretched, his probing fingers encountering nothing but cold, dark air.

His right foot kicked something. It sounded like wood. He crouched down, and his hand came in contact with dried bush and some branches. These at once made him think of a fire. What a relief a bit of light would be!

Paul reached in his pocket and found his waterproof match box still safe. Despite his situation, he smiled wryly at how Chet often had kidded him about having it with him at all times. His fingers trembled a little as he opened it. The matches were still dry, and in a second he struck one and it flared into life.

"Better to light one candle than curse the darkness," Paul grimly said to himself.

The flame, held just under the driest brush, roared out of the heap in a mushroom of fire. The light illuminated the cavern, casting a ruddy glare and writhing shadows on the rocks and the rippling water. It was a weird and uncanny scene, causing him to shiver involuntarily. He would give a good deal to have been in the upper world once more.

More sticks and brush lay scattered about, which probably floated in when the stream flooded, and became stranded on the rocks when the water receded. He shuttled around, gathering the fuel and dumping on the flames until he built a respectable fire. Paul huddled next to it and called on his logic to examine his situation.

He was trapped between a rock and a hard place, quite literally. Allen and Chet would miss him if he was overdue coming home, he was certain about that. They would search for him; maybe even think Grady's men had snatched him. Even if they trailed him to the edge of the gorge, what could they do? Follow the river underground like he did? Or give him up for lost? He knew the odds of his brothers finding him here were low. Sadness welled up inside of him at the thought of never seeing Allen and Chet again. No, he refused to believe that. The truth of the situation was stark, but obvious: if he didn't find away out on his own, he didn't get out. Paul took stock of the surrounding area.

The river had simply widened at the spot, and a hundred yards farther on it flowed into a narrow channel, as before. Only on the side which he occupied held the shape of a shore. The dry land narrowed to not more than thirty feet across at its broadest point. Rocks backed it up. Opposite, the rocks stood straight up, covered with moss and slime.

"If I am to get out," he corrected himself, "to find the way out, it must be from this side upward. I can never get back on the river. One could never row even a boat against that current."

By the flickering light, Paul was glad to see that the rocks on his side of the cavern did not present an unbroken surface. The wall contained numerous fissures, and in one case the opening appeared to be more than ten feet wide. This told him where to go—the only direction possible.

Chapter 7

Paul scoured the rocky area for all the burnable things he could find. He selected one branch, about three feet long. Unsnapping his Bowie knife from its holder, he sliced grooves into the top of the wood, then resheathed his blade. He stuffed smaller twigs and brush into the notches, then put that end of the limb into the fire until it ignited. Picking it up as a torch in one hand, Paul also selected a couple of the longer sticks as backups to hold in his other hand. He left the vicinity of the stream and started to explore the gap in the rock wall. He hoped it would lead upward and would enable him to climb out of his potential tomb—for to him that damp, dark place was just that, nothing more or less. The torch flickered and sputtered in the thick, stagnant air.

Stones, ranging in size from that of a pebble to that of a human head, littered the opening. Paul tread carefully, so as not to trip and send himself tumbling onto the rocky ground. The last thing he needed was a sprained ankle, or worse. He moved along with caution, halting every few steps to survey the scene ahead and make sure of his footing. The air in the fissure was thick and dank, and it clung to Paul's skin like a second layer.

About sixty feet from the entrance to the fissure, Paul came to a turn to the left. In the flickering gloom, he spotted an opening just big enough for him to squeeze through. It led to another cavern, not over ten yards in width and height of interminable length.

Fearful of losing his way, Paul hesitated about advancing. But presently he decided he couldn't go back, so he had no other choice for now. He plucked up courage, and, holding down his firebrand, he allowed it to burn up again and then proceeded along the chamber.

The floor of the cavern was uneven, and Paul tested each footstep. Huge stalactites hung down from overhead, like daggers ready to spear him, and in several spots the moisture dripped down with weird hollow sounds, making him feel more lonely and lost than ever. In the center of the chamber was a pool of water, its surface still and glassy. It looked like a black mirror, reflecting back the chamber and all its wonders.

The firebrand illuminated the way, but it also created deep shadows that made it difficult to see. The chamber seemed to go on forever. Paul's throat was dry, and his head was starting to throb.

"I wonder how far underground I really am." Paul's natural curiosity exerted itself even now, and he tried to use it to force the thoughts of fear out of his head. He came to a halt beside a tiny stream which flowed from one side of the cavern to the other. "If I could find some slope which led upward it would be more encouraging. But it's about as flat as a bit of prairie land."

Paul hopped over the water, and, assured that he could easily retrace his steps if necessary, continued his search, his torch held over his head.

He let out a groan when he reached the end of the cave. His voice echoed off the walls and sounded muffled to his own ears. Before him arose a solid wall not less than twenty feet in height, at which elevation the cavern appeared to continue. Paul gazed up at the barrier with a hopeless look on his face.

How in the name of creation am I to climb up there? he wondered. The rock was as steep as the side of a house and twice as slippery. He needed to find some sort of handholds or footholds. If he couldn't...

He didn't want to finish that thought. It would mean defeat and a slow death.

Waving the firebrand to make it burn the brighter, Paul began to scrutinize the face of the wall before him. He started at one end, resolved that not a foot of the surface should escape him.

Paul cast his eyes about for some means of scaling the rock. He walked along its face until he reached the very side, and there, to his joy, discovered what appeared to be a dozen rudely cut niches, some of them were close together and others about a yard apart.

"I must not have been the first to make this journey," he said out loud, the cave repeating his words. He couldn't tell how long ago the cuts were made, but their mere presence buoyed his spirits somewhat, although he hoped he didn't stumble across the skeleton of the other unfortunate explorer at the top.

The niches were just big enough for him to put his foot in and boost himself up. He tested the first one and found it to be sturdy. With a deep breath, he started to climb, awkwardly carrying his burdens with him. The going was slow and painstaking. Finally, he pulled himself up to the flooring of the cavern above.

Paul now found himself in an opening not over fifty yards square. The roofing was hardly out of reach, and the young man saw at a glance that it was quartz rock, shot through with silver and gold colored veins. Despite the beauty of what was over him, the thought of escape came back. Did this branch of the cave lead to a route to the outside, or was he entombed alive?

"Stop thinking that," he ordered himself, as he picked up the branches and started walking again. He forced himself to recall some of Ike's outlandish stories, causing him to smile. "I'll better him with this tale. And this one is true."

At the far end of the chamber, after a long search, Paul came to a narrow passageway, which required him to enter on hands and knees. It sloped upward and hope grew that before long he would emerge into the outer air once more.

At the far end of the chamber Paul came to a narrow passageway, which required him to enter on hands and knees. It sloped upward at a gradual incline, and hope grew within him that before long he would emerge into the outer air once more.

The passage led around numerous curves. He crawled on, his knees and palms raw from the rough ground, feeling the walls pressing in on him, but he pushed onward. He handled the torch clumsily, pushing, then dragging, the extra sticks and once almost left them behind, but for some unknown reason didn't. He turned another corner and groaned in frustration.

The cave forked in two directions. He stopped, unsure of which way to go. One path seemed as good as the other, but he didn't know if one would lead to freedom or if it would take him deeper into the earth. He didn't know which path to choose, unsure of what he would find.

The orange and red flames of his torch flickered. It was feeble, but it was a draft! Air was blowing through the right-hand tunnel! It was dank and dark, but the ghost of fresh air, as slight as it felt, was a sign that there was an exit.

He followed the right-hand passage until it brought him against a solid wall at last. Frightened, he looked around. Except behind him, the rocks arose straight up on all sides, almost like a chimney, but overhead was open.

Another whisper of air fanned the torch. The only direction it could be coming from was above. As best he was able, he examined the opening at the roof of the room he stood in. It appeared that another shaft crossed the top of the fissure, like a letter 'T', leading off to the right and the left. One of those directions must connect to the outside, the source of the breeze.

Paul stuck his torch in a small crack in the floor and put down the other wood. He checked the walls for any hand holds, hoping to discover others like before. But nothing marred the smooth rock wall.

He estimated the top of the room at maybe twelve feet tall. Coiling himself up into a spring, he leaped into the air and made a grab for the edge of the opening. Not high enough.

Concentrating on his goal, Paul jumped again. Another miss, as was a third attempt. Paul gave vent to his frustration with a scream. It echoed off the rock, mocking him.

"Rope, I need a rope," he said to himself. "Think, think."

His holster was too heavy, his belt too short … He paced around the small diameter of the cave until the idea came to him. Smiling, he sat down and pulled out his Bowie knife. Taking off his shirt, he used the blade to cut and tear it into strips, then tied the pieces into two ribbons. He tethered one end of each length of cloth to the thickest limb he brought with him, then twisted the fabric and knotted the ends together to secure them.

Paul stood, slipped his knife back into its holder and admired his handiwork. He picked up the stick, and heaved it, like a spear, toward the opening in the roof. One end crossed the lip, but the other one didn't, and the whole thing dropped back to the ground.

He threw his contraption again and again, varying the angle and the speed of his throws. He aimed it at different spots and twirled it in the air so that it seemed to spin around its center, and continuing to make more adjustments. After uncounted tries, the stick wedged both ends on top of the opening, the knotted cloth hanging down.

Paul leaped again, grabbed the material and lifted his feet; it supported his weight. He climbed his way up, hand over hand, panting with exertion and triumph. His makeshift climbing rope held. When he reached the branch, he pulled himself up and swung his legs up on the edge of the intersecting passage. He paused a moment to catch his breath, and then gingerly maneuvered himself until he was able to sit on the surface of the upper level.

He grinned. The air was definitely fresher up here. And, unless he was very much mistaken, he could make out a glimmer of daylight down one connection.

The shaft was low, forcing him to remain on his hands and knees. The rock walls fell away, and he wriggled, dug, pushed, and kicked his way higher through weeds and brush and dirt toward the light, toward life. He scraped his elbow and grazed his knee as he continued to climb. His muscles burned and began to weaken.

He was ready to give up in despair, when another breath of cool, sweet air blew over him. It carried the welcome scent of sage and gave him the strength he needed to carry on. He climbed harder than ever, up and up he went until suddenly opening his eyes, he found himself at the top of the hole and looking almost directly into the face of the sun!

A large sage spread over the exit. Paul wriggled out and shoved his way through the plant, in a final push to the freedom of the outside. The bush scratched at his face, hands and chest like a hundred little claws.

He burst into the sunlight like a mole coming out of its burrow. Running forward a few steps, his arms held up to the glorious sun and laughed. He spun around, then dropped to the dirt. He pointed to the sky.

"I knew you were logical!" he called out. He took a deep breath, savoring the air as a starving man before a meal. "Heaven be thanked for my escape!" murmured Paul to himself. "All night underground!"

The climb so exhausted him that for a long while he rested on the ground, unable to move. He felt both cold and hungry, but paid no heed. He was outside at last. After a while, he sat up, and surveyed his surroundings.

He was in a small depression, shaped like a bowl. The rocky walls slopped up on all sides in a jagged way, rocks and boulders littered the floor, making the hollow look like an abandoned mine. The sage was the only plant in the area, appearing as if it had wandered in here by mistake.

One crag in particular caught his attention: tall, made of layers of different type of rock. He gazed at it for a full minute, admiring the sight before putting his natural curiosity aside and turning back to the task at hand: to figure out where he was as well as how far he would have to travel to reach the ranch. The face of the country appeared new and strange to him. For a second, he hoped he hadn't somehow ended up on a piece of Captain Grady's land. Being discovered there would certainly cause more problems.

"No, I reckon it's all right," he said to himself. "The next best thing is to strike out for home. To the south."

Paul felt stronger, and he used the rocks to climb his way up one of the sides. At the top, he saw hills, populated with scattered pines, folding away in every direction.

He needed a higher vantage point. He climbed up a formidable slope toward the top on the highest ridge. It was tough going, and he decided to only focus on reaching a specific tree or rock, one at a time, not on thinking about the summit. It broke the ascent up into more manageable pieces. He began to sing to distract himself from his fatigue, estimating how much farther he had to go by the number of verses he'd need to reach a particular landmark ahead. When he finally gained the hilltop at last, he scanned the area in surprise. It didn't look as steep from there as it did when he was climbing it, and a portion of the river ravine where he began his adventure was visible in the distance. There were only a few ridges in between.

Paul took his bearings and then struck off as rapidly as his tired legs and sore feet would permit. In a few hours, he reached the canyon where the river disappeared underground. He followed the gorge back to where he started his adventure, although keeping a safe distance from edge this time. He found his gun in the dirt where he had dropped it before taking his tumble over the cliff, holstered it and looked around.

"Jasper!" he called. He waited a second, whistled, then shouted again. "Jasper!"

An answering neigh came from the nearby stand of woods. His animal emerged from under the trees and trotted toward him. Paul beamed.

"I always said you were sometimes more dog than horse," Paul laughed as he stroked Jasper's muzzle. He gratefully climbed into the saddle and took the reins. "Let's go home."

Chapter 8

Allen sat at his father's desk, the fanciest piece of furniture in the house. The ranch's account book lay open in front of him, along with a few other papers. He glumly stared at the columns of figures marching down the page.

He had been there most of the morning. His thoughts and worries circled around in his mind like a corral of wild horses. Allen didn't know how to deal with Captain Grady's immense threat: it was about taking everything away from them. Their property, their livelihood, their home. Everything their family had worked for years to build would be gone just like that. They had no cash to hire an attorney to fight Grady if it came down to that. Allen knew he couldn't fix the money problem; he didn't have any solutions for the stolen savings either. They had some cattle ready for sale, but no way to pay to ship them. The three brothers could drive their herd all the way to the market by themselves perhaps, but it would be very difficult and leave their place unattended, allowing Grady a potential opening to move in. Selling the herd to an agent would only bring a fraction of the cattle's real worth, and most likely not as much as their usual amount. Even with less money than usual, they may be able to operate the spread, but if Grady sued them, all their cash would have to go to fight him in court, bringing Allen back to the captain's threats. These worries kept piling up, higher and higher, heavier and heavier.

His stomach churned, as if his insides were being crushed, like being packed inside a preserve jar. He drummed his pencil on the desk, a frenzied rhythm that matched the way his brain spun around the problems in his head. He looked frantically from one side of his desk to the other, searching for something on the papers in front of him that would give him an idea, but encountered nothing. Usually when he saw an obstacle in front of him, he'd take it as a challenge to cross it. Not this time. The barrier appearing before him appeared too big to surmount.

One word, bright red and large, loomed over everything: failure. Allen's failing in his promise to his father to keep the family together and hang on to their home.

Chet understood the unspoken rule of not disturbing Allen when he worked at the desk, and so he spent the morning attending to his chores around the barn. Around noon, Chet's voice rang from the outside, breaking into Allen's thoughts.

"Paul! What happened to you?"

Allen swung around in his chair as his brothers entered through the front door. Paul was filthy, shirtless, wore no hat, and was scratched. He trudged along, Chet following.

"Are you all right?" Chet asked.

Paul nodded. "Only tired and hungry."

"I'll get you—" Chet started.

"Well?" Allen's curt voice cut him off. "What happened? Was it Grady's men?"

Paul shook his head and managed a weary smile. "No. I can't blame this on Grady."

Allen's eyes drilled into Paul. "What? Did Jasper dust you?"

"No, he didn't throw me." Paul plopped in a chair with a groan. After taking a deep breath, he told Allen and Chet of his encounter with the bear, falling into the river and his escape from the cave.

For Allen, it was too much, one thing too many. The morning's tension, so tightly packed in him, had to go somewhere. Allen's face turned red and his chest heaved. Paul's story lit a match to a powder keg in Allen's stomach.

"One thing! I ask for one thing! One simple thing!" Allen exploded. "Keep an eye on the range so Grady doesn't come over, and you fall into Black Rock River!"

"Allen, I told you, there was a bear—" Paul started.

"I know! I heard you! Didn't you have your gun?" Allen yelled. He realized he was wrong shouting at Paul like this, but he couldn't control himself. All the frustration of the morning spewed out like a geyser, but it was Paul's misfortune to be in the way. "Shoot the bear!"

Paul stood, and spoke in an even, controlled tone. "Allen, I didn't want to unless—"

"Shoot the damn bear!" Allen jumped to his feet. "Oh, I know, you thought 'I don't want to kill this nice friendly grizzly, so I'll plunge over the edge the cliff instead.' And you're supposed to be the smart one in the family!"

Paul walked up to Allen and placed one hand on Allen's shoulder. He spoke softly. "Allen, please, you're being unreasonable—"

Allen didn't want Paul's calm demeanor now; it was the last thing he could tolerate. It only made him more irate. He brushed off Paul's hand. "Do I have to do everything around here? Don't I have enough on my mind as it is? Don't I have enough to worry about other than to wonder if you'll fall off into a ravine the moment I let you out of my sight?"

All Allen wanted to do now was smash Paul's placid composure into a million pieces. It was the one thing—no, the most important thing—he could accomplish and the one thing he could succeed at this instant. It was the one barrier he could cross. "Is it? Well, is it? Am I asking too much?"

"At least I didn't almost get lynched," Paul spat back.

"What? Who almost got lynched?" Chet shouted.

Allen shot a furious look toward Chet then jabbed a finger in Paul's face and growled. "I told you never to talk about that."

"What's happening? What's all this about? Will somebody tell me?" Chet cried.

"Why shouldn't I mention it?" Paul challenged. "Because you would be dead, hanging from a tree if Ike hadn't rescued you? Because Allen the Great can't do everything all by himself? Because it means maybe, just maybe, our big brother sometimes needs our help, but doesn't want to give up an ounce of control to ask for it?"

Allen backhanded Paul across the mouth. It was a forceful blow. Paul grunted at its impact and staggered a few steps to his left. For a moment, the only sound came from metallic ticking of the mantle clock. Paul took a breath, and returned to his position, standing directly in front of Allen.

Although his brother's hands were balled into fists, Allen knew he wouldn't strike back. That only increased Allen frustration. He drew back his fist and grabbed Paul's right shoulder.

Chet latched on Allen's arm. Allen winced at the strength of Chet's grip. "Stop it, Allen! No! No!"

With some difficulty, Allen shook off Chet like he would a small, yapping dog. He snarled at Paul. "All right, all right, be the big man! Go ahead and tell him everything!"

Turning on his heel, Allen strode out the front door, kicking a chair out of the way en route. Outside, the bright sunlight stung his eyes, momentarily blinding him. He didn't stop moving. When his sight cleared, he found himself on the way to the river.

Emotions swirled inside his head like a cyclone. Anger, shame at hitting Paul, embarrassment at losing his temper, anxiety about Grady, the ranch, the stolen money, the brothers' future, or their lack of one. Everything about him was crumbling, disintegrating; his world was collapsing into a pile of rubble right in front of him. He felt trapped in a box canyon with no way out; he didn't know what to do, where to start. He saw his father standing in front of him, a ghost visible even in the harsh afternoon sun, not angry, because he rarely lost his temper, but gazing at Allen in sad disappointment, as if let down.

Failure.

Allen reached the river's edge. He leaned his back against the tree and slid down until he sat on the ground. Pulling his knees up, he hugged them, holding himself. He rocked back and forth as he listened to the sound of water as it gently gurgled by. Footsteps came up behind him, but he was too agitated to care who it was.

"Allen..." It was Paul.

"Go away!" Allen moaned out angrily, dropping his forehead to his knees.

"Chet's upset."

"Leave me alone!" Allen barked each word.

"Of course." Paul replied in a quiet voice after a pause. He left.

The river's serene water gurgled by. A few bird songs floated through the hot air, joined by the buzzing of some insects. Allen lifted his head, his face devoid of any expression. The silence was so deep Allen heard his own breath, which seemed to echo into a dark distance. Something appeared to fill the void.

He began to weep.

***

The atmosphere in the house grew unpleasant and tense in the days following the argument between Allen and Paul. Allen retreated into a moody, irritable silence, barely grunting one-word responses to any speech directed toward him. Paul tried to speak with him but was rebuffed so much that he finally gave up. The pair just ignored each other, two thunderclouds waiting to collide and set off the storm. That morning, Paul and Chet awoke to discover a terse note from Allen saying he was going to ride the property.

"I'm surprised he didn't add that he wouldn't end up in the river," Paul sarcastically muttered as he crumpled up the paper.

Even with Allen gone, Paul remained glum. Chet decided he had to get away from the place for a time, no matter how long or short. He needed to do something, not just wait for Allen and Paul to come to blows, although he almost wished that would happen. At least it would clear the air. He hoped.

Chet announced his own journey: he was going to Daddy Wampole's to check if a letter from Uncle Barnaby had arrived.

Paul merely nodded, as if only half-listening, as he discarded the wadded up paper into the stove's firebox.

It was twenty miles to Daddy Wampole's hotel; a direct route would not make it over ten, but Chet couldn't fly as the birds do. Several hills to climb and half dozen water courses to ford were in his path. It meant hours in the saddle, but he didn't mind it.

Chet left the ranch as quickly as possible, taking advantage of the early morning coolness while the sun still sat low over the horizon. He passed the level stretch outside the ranch's border and came to a good-sized brook. Beyond was a belt of timber and the first of the hills.

He watered Rush, took a drink himself, and pushed on without stopping longer. Chet knew he must keep on the move if he wanted to arrive at the Crossroads Hotel before the late afternoon.

On through the forest of spruce and hemlock, with here and there a tall cottonwood, he spurred his horse. The foot of a hill was soon reached, and up he toiled. Around noon Chet halted near the crest of a second rise. He had brought jerked meat and crackers from home which comprised a comfortable, but not luxurious, meal. Even though he sat by himself, it really wasn't any different from how meals were around the house the last couple of days. After saying grace, the brothers would lapse into an uneasy silence, the only sounds coming from utensils scrapping the dishes as the three simply stared at their plates as they ate.

In thirty minutes, Chet and Rush were again on the way, the horse having also been fed in the meantime. It was now the hottest part of the day. The way was dry and dusty and Rush hung out his tongue as he walked on. Chet was relieved when he reached a portion of the road overhung by huge rocks a hundred feet or more in height. Some rude structures shimmered in the sunlight below: the Crossroads Hotel. Chet smiled. The sight of the buildings raised his spirits. He had less than a mile to go.

Daddy Wampole's land stood at the junction of two major roads. After the stage began to run along them, he gave up ranching when he discovered he could make more money tending people than cattle.

Off Chet went on a gallop. In ten minutes he drew up at the horse block and dismounted. Old Daddy Wampole, a well-known character throughout that part of the state, came out on the porch of his house-turned-hotel to greet him.

"Hey, Chet!" he called out. "Yer jest in time. New mail came in."

"From last week's late stage, or was this week's early?" Chet asked with a laugh.

Wampole let out a guffaw. "Don't know, son, don't know. That stage's schedule is more of a suggestion."

They stepped through the doorway of the ranch house. One room did duty as a general store, barroom, and also served as the area's post office, which consisted of a box mounted on the wall. The incoming letters and packages went into it and whoever wanted to could pick them out. Another soap box, hung lower, was reserved for anything outgoing. The post came down from Deadwood once a week or so on the stage.

Chet stopped as the hotel owner walked toward an open door. "I'll fetch the mail. It's mixed up with some liquor sent down."

Wampole disappeared through the doorway. Chet glanced around the stuffed room. Shelves lined every wall, loaded with a variety of items: food cans, kerosene lamps, bolts of cloth, men's jeans and boots, rifles and bullets, and a single fluffy woman's hat, the attached large white feather shifting in the warm breeze blowing in from the open door. On another wall, one shelf held liquor bottles and glasses, with a board resting on two barrels in front serving as the bar. Chet spotted an edition of *Leslie's Illustrated Newspaper*. He grabbed the periodical.

"Say, Daddy, can I have this magazine?" Chet called.

"For Paul?" Wampole stepped back into the room, holding several letters in one hand. "Surely. It's more than a couple of months old, I think."

Chet leafed through the pages and laughed. "Paul won't care."

Wampole held out one letter to Chet, then dumped the few others in the soap box. "Here's one for your Uncle Barnaby. All the way from San Francisco."

With great effort, Chet resisted the urge to snatch the paper out of Wampole's hand. He casually took it. "Thanks, Daddy."

Chet stepped out the front door and closed it. He clamped the magazine under one arm and got ready to tear open the envelope. Just then, two men rode up and dismounted. They stomped up the stairs to the porch.

"Quit yer complaining," the first men snapped to the second. "Hey, cheer up! Yer old warden may have written to you."

"Har, har. Very funny, Saul," groused the other. "Spending our time watchin' for some fellow's letters from San Fran—"

The slamming door cut off the rest of the sentence. Chet heard the rumble of voices from inside but couldn't understand the words.

Mail from San Francisco? He looked at the letter in his hand. Anybody could be mailed something from there. Why had those two men just stopped by the hotel? And why today, of all days? It could be just coincidence, but ... Chet shook his head. He didn't think it likely. Did those two men know anything about his missing uncle? Perhaps he could find out.

He slipped the envelope inside the *Leslie's Illustrated*. He strolled past the window and glanced in. The two men stood at the bar, drinking whiskey. Chet sat on the edge of the porch and pretended to read as he waited.

After about five minutes, the men stumped out of the ranch house, and back to their horses. Chet slyly watched them out of the corner of his eye. One man looked at Chet's horse and seemed to recognize it. He glanced toward Chet, who continued to act engrossed in what he read. Then the two men got on their mounts and started to ride away unhurriedly.

Chet walked to Rush, stuffing the magazine and letter inside his saddle bag. Climbing onto his horse, he began to follow the other two men, who were just rounding a curve in the trail, passing behind a clump of trees. As he also made the turn, the other two men were still visible ahead. Chet reined in Rush to stay what he thought was a safe distance back. His targets passed out of sight behind another stand of cottonwoods. Chet sped up slightly and headed around the trees.

"Hold it!" ordered a gruff voice. It was accompanied by the chilling clicking of two guns cocking.

Chet stopped. The two men rode out from their hiding place in trees, each one coming up on either side of Chet, pistols drawn.

"Hi, fellas." Chet tried to cover the quiver in his voice, but failed. "What's all this about?"

"We don't like bein' followed, that's what, youngster," said one man.

"Following you?" Chet gave a halfhearted laugh. "Shoot, I'm going the same way as you, that's all."

"If that be true, let's just keep company a spell," said the second man. "How about it, Darry?"

"Mighty good idea, Saul. Glad for the company," agreed the first man. He waved his gun. "Get goin'."

Chet swallowed hard and started to ride, sandwiched between Saul and Darry, both guns still trained on him.

The trio rode silently for a while, until they came to a fork in the trail. They stopped.

"Well, this is where I go," Chet said, pointing to the trail going off to the right. He had no idea where it went, but he was going to take it, anyway.

"Nah, I think we'll all go the other way," drawled Saul.

"I'm expected back home," Chet tried. "If I don't come back, they'll send out people to search."

Saul responded by directing Chet with his gun to the left trail. The three continued for a while.

"Far enough," Saul said. He dismounted. "Get down, boy."

Chet got off Rush.

"Get rid of the horse, Darry." Saul jerked his head toward Chet's mount.

Darry took Rush's reins and trotted back toward the fork. Chet heard a slap, and Rush galloping back the way they came.

"What's this about? I don't have any money. I'm not armed," Chet said. Saul didn't respond. Darry rode up behind Chet. He tried again. "I wasn't following you. Honest."

"We don't quite believe you, Darry and me," Saul said. "We think we needs to teach you a lesson on how unfriendly it is to track folks, don't we, Darry?"

"That we do." Darry slid off his horse in back of Chet and pinned his arms behind him. Chet struggled. "Hey, yer pretty strong for a such young pup. Better tie him tight, Saul."

Saul pulled a length of rope off his horse's saddle and stood in front of Chet. "Hold up your hands."

Darry released Chet. He put out his wrists, and Saul tied them together with one end of the rope. The man climbed on his mount, gripping the other end of the lead. He grinned at Chet, then spurred his mount into a trot.

The horse took off, and the slack of the line ran out. It almost jerked Chet off his feet. He began to jog behind Saul, trying not to fall.

"How's he doin'?" Saul called out.

"Tolerable," replied Darry.

Saul's horse went into a canter. Chet yelped and was pulled after him. He tripped, almost fell but regained his footing again in an instant, gaining speed as he raced behind Saul.

Darry's animal galloped in and caught up to Saul. The two men nodded at each other. Saul tossed the rope to Darry, who veered away, pulling Chet off balance to run in a different direction. Darry and Saul kept it up, seeming for hours, hooting and hollering as they passed the rope to each other, whipping Chet into one way, then another, then yet another, forcing him to keep running. Chet was gasping and heaving for breath, like he were drowning in the open air, trying to stay on his feet. His legs ached and felt as if they were being driven into his skull with every step. Perspiration drenched him.

Darry's horse broke into a gallop. Chet couldn't keep his footing any longer and stumbled, fell and was dragged through the dirt for a short time, sliding to a stop only when Darry released his grip on the rope. Chet sprawled on the ground, gasping like a landed fish about to be gutted. Darry and Saul walked over to him, kicking dirt balls. Saul used his boot to turn Chet over on his back as if a dead animal.

"School's out," Saul sneered. "Have you learnt yer lesson?"

Chet nodded. Saul yanked Chet's hair to pull him upright. Darry looped the remaining rope around Chet's torso, tying his arms to his sides, then let him flop to the ground. Saul and Darry mounted their horses and galloped out of the clearing, roaring with laughter. Chet struggled for air, his chest rising and falling against the ropes. He had to get back on the main trail. It was getting dark now, but he didn't want to wait for the moon to come out so he could see. He felt his muscles stiffen as he stood, his legs still aching from running.

Chet shambled along mindlessly, his shuffling feet mechanically stirring up dust and kicking stones. Every step hurt, but he forced himself to ignore the pain. His legs burned, and he screamed at them to stop complaining and to keep moving forward. Stumbling. he fell to his knees but forced himself back up and continued.

He dropped a second time. He swayed, then pitched face first into the dirt.

Chapter 9

Paul gazed out the open window in a room at Daddy Wampole's hotel, tugging at his shirt collar as he tried to snag even a whisper of a breeze. After a moment, he gave up and turned around.

Allen sat in a straight-backed chair by a bed in which Chet slept. For some reason, his younger brother appeared even smaller, almost shriveled, under the covers. More minutes dribbled by until Chet at last stirred and opened his eyes. For a second, he didn't seem to recognize where he was.

"You're in a room at Daddy Wampole's hotel," Paul explained as he walked to stand behind Allen. He grinned. "It's about time you woke up. You spent the whole morning sleeping."

"What happened now, Chet?" Allen's voice was heavy with weariness, but still cut with sharpness.

Chet reacted to Allen's tone. "I'm feeling much better now, thank you for asking."

Allen stiffened. Paul reached down and put one hand on Allen's shoulder. His older brother's muscles were tense and knotted under his shirt. Paul tossed a meaningful glance toward Chet. "Allen, perhaps Chet would like some water."

Chet caught the hint. "Yes. Yes, Allen, I would like some water, please. I'm awfully thirsty."

Allen grunted a response, got up and left the room. Chet watched him go, muttering something angrily under his breath.

"He hasn't budged from that chair since we got here. He's been worried about you," Paul said.

"Well, he sure has a funny way of showing it," Chet grumbled. He thought of something. "Rush?"

"He's in the barn," Paul said. "We can thank him for how you were found. Rush wandered back here alone, so Daddy knew there was something amiss. A couple of local ranchers were at the bar, so Daddy rounded them up and they all searched. Fortunately, they had enough of a moon to see. They came across you at the junction of the main road and the trail to Jordan Creek."

"I don't remember getting that far," Chet mumbled.

"One of the men even rode all the way out to our place to tell Allen and I. We got here around 3 o'clock in this morning," Paul went on.

Chet propped himself up on his elbows. "What about the letter?"

"Letter?" Allen stood in the door, holding a cup. He walked to the bed and gave it to Chet. "What letter?"

"Thank you, Allen." Chet sipped the water. He continued excitedly. "I found one addressed to Uncle Barnaby. Check in Rush's saddlebag, inside the magazine."

Paul began toward the door. "I'll go. Tell Allen what happened to you. You can tell me later."

He darted down the stairs, two at a time, and hurried into the kitchen. A boiling pot of coffee rested on the stove in preparation for the stage's afternoon arrival. Daddy lifted the lid from the pot, the dark-brown liquid bubbled and boiled, and the scent of roasted beans spilled out.

"Chet awake yet?" Daddy replaced the top and counted some spoons out from a drawer.

"Yes," Paul smiled. "He doesn't appear to be worse for the wear."

Daddy grinned back. "Good. He's a strong one, that boy."

"Daddy, how can we thank you—" Paul started.

"That's about the fifteenth time you've asked me!" Daddy laughed and waved off the thanks. He pulled some mugs off a shelf. "Everybody needs to look out for everybody out here."

"Yes, I know, but thanks—"

Daddy brandished a coffee mug over his head. "Paul, if you say 'thanks' one more time, I gonna brain you with one of these!"

Paul held up his hands in mock surrender. "All right! All right! You win! Done! I'll stop!"

He jogged to the barn located just behind Daddy's house. Rummaging through the bag on Rush's saddle, he pulled out the *Illustrated News*. He flipped thorough the pages and extracted the letter. He trotted back to Chet's room.

"They sound like the horse thieves I encountered, all right," Allen was saying as Paul came in. Allen shook his head. "Why did you follow them?"

"It seemed like a good idea at the time," Chet weakly responded.

Paul smiled a thanks to Chet as he held up the *Leslie's Illustrated News.*

"I thought you would like it," Chet grinned back.

Paul handed the letter to Allen.

"Read it," Allen sighed as he gave it back. He slumped forward in the chair, elbows on his knees, and rubbed his face.

Paul opened the envelope and stepped to the window for better light. He unfolded the paper. "It comes from a Mister Noel Urner. The letterhead says that he is a broker and speculator. Looks like he lists offices in New York City and San Francisco. There's also a line about Urner's specialty being mining stocks."

"Uncle Barnaby told us he had discovered something. Maybe he wanted this Urner's help in trying to form a company to develop the new strike," Chet suggested.

"A most definite possibility." Paul nodded. "Perhaps—"

Allen sat up. He prompted irritably. "The letter?"

"Yes, the letter. It reads: 'Dear Mr. Winthrup: I'm sorry we couldn't meet again at your hotel. The clerk at the Gold Nugget House gave me the note which said you had suddenly been called back to your ranch due to an emergency.'" Paul stopped reading and looked up, puzzled. "Emergency? What emergency? Allen, did you write Uncle Barnaby?"

Allen shook his head.

"Well, Mr. Urner says that." Paul shrugged and went back to the text. "'I had pressing business in New York City, and had to leave the next day. I just returned to San Francisco. While back east, I displayed the ore sample you provided to other investors and two are expressing interest. Should you desire to proceed in this matter, please reply to me at this address at your earliest convenience. Yours truly, Noel Urner.'"

The brothers were silent. Allen held out his hand, and Paul gave him the letter and envelope. Allen read it again to himself.

"I am afraid somebody has played Uncle Barnaby foul," said Chet. "If he had left San Francisco of his own accord, we would have heard from him by now."

"As much as I hate to agree with you, it sure looks like it," Paul said. "Why should Uncle Barnaby leave the hotel in that way if all was perfectly fine? We didn't send a message about any emergency."

"Wouldn't uncle know our writing?" Chet asked.

"For sure your chicken scratching, Chet," Paul returned. He thought a second. "Perhaps the false letter said it was from our neighbor Mr. Dottery, telling we were all sick with the fever or something and couldn't manage ourselves. Uncle wouldn't recognize his handwriting."

"Do you think uncle mentioned his discovery to other people?" Chet wondered. "I mean, he wouldn't even tell us much."

"Many a man lost the chance of his lifetime by advertising his knowledge too broadly. Others could gain a clue of a mine, hunt it up, and stake the claim before the original discoverer knew what happened. Possibly some mining town rascals got hold of his secret and put him out of the way, so they might profit by the information," reasoned Paul. "There are plenty of fellows mean enough for that."

"Just my idea, too," said Chet. "The question is, who met him in San Francisco, and what did they do?"

"Well, it couldn't have been Mr. Urner." Paul went back to the window. "Why would he send that message if he had a hand in Uncle Barnaby's disappearance? That doesn't make sense."

"So we've moved a little more in one direction, but are no farther down the road," Chet spoke in a soft voice.

Allen still stared at the letter as silence filled the room again. Finally, he folded the paper, slipped it back in the envelope, and tucked it away in his coat pocket. He stood.

"I'm going to leave immediately," Allen announced.

"Leave? To where?" asked Paul in astonishment.

Allen walked to the door. "Direct to San Francisco to hunt up tidings of Uncle Barnaby."

"You must be fooling!" Chet blurted out.

"Never more serious in my life, Chet," Allen replied firmly. "I feel my duty is to discover what happened to uncle, if possible, at once. With Mr. Urner's name and office location, as well as the hotel's name, at least those are two places to begin to inquire."

"Well, yes, but, Allen, it's such a journey—" Paul began.

"Do either of you two have a better idea?" Allen snapped. He waited a second. "Well?"

"No," Paul admitted. Chet shook his head.

"I'm not anxious to take this trip, but there is no other choice at present. I'll ride to the nearest station on the railroad, which is not isn't over a hundred and forty miles, and then take the train. The journey on the cars will not take over a couple of days, all told." Allen turned to leave.

"How are you going to pay for the ticket?" Paul framed his question as gently as he could. Although he was pleased to see some of Allen's fire return, he didn't want to make him angry again, so Paul employed all his diplomacy as he could.

Allen spun around and glared at Paul. "What did you say?"

Paul wasn't sure if Allen was irritated at Paul for his question or if he was upset at himself because he hadn't considered it before. Paul broke off eye contact and looked at the floor. He took a breath, repeating the question in calmest voice that he could muster. "I asked, how are you going to pay for the ticket?"

"Paul's right," Chet added gently, "those thieves took all our money. We have nothing."

The rattling and creaking of the approaching stage, the shouting of the driver and the thundering of the team's hooves drifted into the room. Allen stood in the doorway, head down, shoulders slumped, arms hanging limply at his side. His eyes were unfocused and his face was blank and motionless. Paul had never seen a person appear so utterly defeated and empty.

The stagecoach halted in front of Daddy Wampole's place, his raucous greeting splitting the still, hot afternoon air, the sound of the horses' breaths steamed through the heat. The noise of the talking passengers getting off the stage and pounding into the hotel sounded so normal, so alive, the subdued scene in the bedroom seemed to be taking place in another world.

After a few minutes, Allen took a deep breath. He stood erect, squaring his shoulders. He looked directly at Paul. "I will sell Lily."

"No!" Both Paul and Chet cried, immediately offering their horses to be sold instead.

"Discussion ended!" Allen was adamant. "I will sell Lily. She's a good mare and should fetch a fair price. I will make it do with what I get. I will buy a cut-rate ticket from Ogden, if I can." He pointed at Paul and barked out commands. "When Chet feels better, head back to the ranch. Do nothing but guard the cattle and the place generally. Try to stay out of trouble, both of you. I'll be back, or I'll let you hear from me just as soon as I can. In case you need anything, go to Dottery's place. I'm sure he'll help you."

He stared at Paul and Chet, almost like a general appraising his troops after giving a command. He turned to leave.

"Allen ... " Paul started.

Allen stopped and looked back over his shoulder.

"Best of luck," Paul said.

Allen responded with the slightest of nods and left, shutting the door behind him.

"Do you think he'll find out what happened to Uncle Barnaby?" Chet ventured after a pause.

Paul shrugged. "I don't know. All we can do is hope. Cross that bridge—"

He stopped and cast a glance at Chet.

"Go ahead and say it," Chet said with a smile. "I won't get mad. I promise.

Paul smiled. "Cross that bridge when we come to it."

"Well, I can't stay in bed all day." Chet threw off the covers after a minute. "Let's get back to the ranch."

After Chet had washed and dressed, the two went downstairs to the kitchen. On the table was a simple meal: stew, a loaf of crusty bread, and an apple cake. Daddy Wampole herded them to the chairs and ordered them to eat.

"Where was Allen gettin' off to?" Daddy gestured off toward the south.

Paul told him of the communication from Urner, and Allen's mission to San Francisco. Daddy let out a slow whistle at the news.

"The phony letter about an emergency must have come from around here." Paul picked up his coffee and took a sip. "I can't think of anywhere else."

"Surely Uncle Barnaby wrote back to us when he got it. He must have," Chet jabbed the air with his fork. "Things like when he planned to arrive, and so forth."

Paul nodded in agreement. "Daddy Wample, do you remember if anybody took a letter from Uncle Barnaby meant for us?"

"Shoot, Paul, I don't pay no attention to who took what piece out of the box." Daddy sat at the table and filled his plate with food.

"Of course not. Sorry," Paul said. He paused, then continued. "Well, do you recall anything odd or unusual about the mail recently? In the last few weeks or months, even?"

"A couple of months ago? That's a long time to remember, Paul." Daddy Wampole thought a moment as he chewed. He swallowed. "One time, Jake Talbert got a letter from his mail order bride, and I had to read it to him. He can't read, you know. Boy, did he turn red!" Daddy chuckled.

Paul grinned in response. "That's not what I had in mind. Anything else out of the ordinary? I don't know, maybe if a person took a lot of it at once?

Daddy looked up at the ceiling for a few seconds. "I recollect Cap'n Grady took almost all of them that came in one day."

"So he took most of the letters, did he?" said Paul, thoughtfully. "How many of them, on a rough guess?"

"I dunno," Daddy rubbed his chin as he stared at the ceiling again. He shrugged. "Seven or eight."

"You can't remember if any of them were for Allen, or any of us?" Paul urged.

"No, I don't recollect that, Paul," said Daddy, "but hold on—do ye suspect the cap'n o' tamperin' with yer mail?"

"I don't believe he is above such an action," bluntly stated Paul.

Daddy leaned across the table and spoke in a confidential tone. "Well, neither do I, privately speakin'." He sat back. "Anyway, he didn't get away with nothin'."

"What do you mean?" Paul asked.

"I walked into the front room, and there stood Cap'n Grady with all the letters in his hand, makin' like he was agonna leave," Daddy recounted, "and he seemed surprised-like when he saw me come in, like he didn't expect me. So he looked real quick at the mail, took one envelope out, and put the rest back. Then the cap'n walked over there to the old place and tore it open. Maybe—"

Daddy didn't need to finish. Paul jumped to his feet and sped across the road to what had in former days been the only house in the section.

It was a simple affair, now worn from years of weather and neglect. Nearby a tall, old tree stood sentinel over the structure, its branches dripping shade on what remained of the roof. Hooks hung empty under the eaves, still waiting for wet coats to dry. A bench sat under the overhanging boards, sometimes used by travelers as a resting place. Many a yarn had been told here, many a "horse deal" talked over and closed. People frequently read their letters in the shade of the old house's porch, littering the ground with bits and pieces of torn paper.

Straight to the bench went Paul, and he stood for a moment, scanning for any shreds of mail. He then searched the floor of the ruin, where the wind had blown a great number of twigs and leaves in from outside. He walked around the house peering in all the corners where more debris lay in piles against the walls, and in them he found a quite a few fragments of papers trapped. He gathered them. After he was sure there were no more left in the area, he returned to the kitchen.

"Well, what have you there?" asked Daddy.

"Nearly fifty scraps of letters," answered Paul. "I must search them over at once."

The group cleared the dining table, and spread out the papers on the large, flat top. Paul set to work sorting out the various shreds. It was a tedious task and Chet assisted him. Suddenly the young ranchman uttered a cry.

"Look! This may part of a letter that for Allen," he said. He held up a scrap which bore the words: "—you and Chet can meet me and Paul—"

"Is it in yer uncle's handwritin'?" questioned Daddy.

"Yes," confirmed Chet as he examined the sliver.

"Then it is likely as not, someone stole yer mail, certainly," said Daddy.

"Exactly what was done!" Paul slapped the fragment on the table. "That makes me wonder—"

Paul stopped short.

"Well, what do you wonder?" Chet checked the paper again.

Paul spoke deliberately. "If Grady took this letter, did he have anything to do with Uncle Barnaby's disappearance?"

"The cap'n is a slick one," put in Daddy Wampole. "I never liked him from the day I first set eyes on him. An' seem' as how he's achin' to grab yer ranch from ye family, why, it ain't surprisin' he took that letter and would do more, if 'twas for his own benefit."

"It won't be for his benefit if we find he is playing such an underhand game," Chet asserted. "He fancies we are only three boys, but he'll find out even youngsters can do something when they are put to it."

"So Grady knew when uncle was coming back. Since he didn't come on a stage …" Paul looked to Daddy for confirmation. Daddy nodded. "Then uncle must have been grabbed in the city, or at the railroad station, or on the way back. I wish I could have found the rest of the letter. I'm sure it was of great importance. It would have told us how Uncle Barnaby was traveling home. We need to ask Grady about this."

"The problem is the cap'n is hard to find," noted Daddy Wampole. "He ain't on his ranch more than a quarter o' his time. Ye know he's as much interested in minin' as he is in ranchin'."

The mention of mines gave a new turn to Paul's thoughts. Had the message from Uncle Barnaby contained any reference to his possible bonanza?

"If he is involved, then Grady will rob Uncle Barnaby as sure as fate," Paul said. He sighed. "Theories only. We can't do anything else right now, not without more information. Let's head back to the ranch, Chet."

Paul and Chet thanked Daddy again, and went out to the barn. After saddling their horses, they started back home, Chet telling Paul what happened to him.

"I'll tell you what I would also like to do," remarked Chet. "I would like to find the chap who cleaned us out of our savings. Why didn't Allen and Ike stop the horse thieves and search them. He must have known they had it."

"He tried. He said they didn't have the money on them," Paul said. "It could mean the men Allen and Ike ran into were only part of the gang, or they hid the cash somewhere. In either case, Allen didn't have an opportunity to find out."

"Saul was one of the two men I tangled with," Chet continued. "The cross we found in the barn belongs to him beyond a doubt. The initials prove that, at least to me. We must watch out for that Mangle, and if we can ever get our hands on him, make him give up our money and then have him locked up."

"It is not so easy to lock up a man when you are miles away from a jail," Paul said in resignation.

"You're right. I hope Allen finds Uncle Barnaby," said Chet. He went on quietly. "Do you know, the more I think of it, the more I become convinced something dreadful has happened to him."

"And that's the way I look at it, too, Chet," Paul said.

"And Captain Grady. He's involved. He needs to be locked up," declared Chet.

"We only have suspicions about Grady, but no evidence," cautioned Paul. "We need more facts."

"What about the mail?"

"We don't know if Grady took that particular letter I found the piece of," Paul answered. "Those men you followed were also on the hunt for mail from San Francisco, you said. It could have been them, on an earlier trip, and Daddy didn't notice them take the letter."

The pair rode on in silence. The sun was sinking in the west, and soon long shadows would be upon them. Dusk fell by the time they reached the trail beside the river and started up toward their home.

The brothers sat straight in their saddles and stared in front of them at the same time. They had come in sight of their ranch house. There on the grass behind the barn lay their belongings in a confused mass—stables, chairs, trunks, clothing, one on top of another. In another hopeless heap were the farming implements from the barn. The two spurred their mounts to the piles of their goods and reined up.

"Our furniture and things!" gasped Chet.

"Grady's dirty work, I warrant!" exclaimed Paul. "He's come here and taken possession during our absence."

Paul was correct, for at that moment Captain Grady appeared on the porch, shotgun in hand. He gazed at the boys without saying a word. The sarcastic smile on the captain's face told plainly he rather enjoyed the situation.

Chapter 10

Allen rode Lily at a slow pace through the hot day. He didn't want to tire her out in the heat, but he knew also this would be the last time he would ever ride her. He smiled at his faithful mare gently and patted her slender neck. She was the best horse ever, and that worsened his sadness. His eyes stung at the thought of the actual moment of having to sell her, and how hard it would be to leave her in the hands of a new owner. He wiped away the traces of tears with the back of his hand.

Although he talked to his brothers with confidence about the journey, he was nervous about it. This would be the first time he had spent any length of time away from home, not to mention the first time he ever set foot on a train. He'd seen the iron horse from the distance, of course, but that didn't mean he knew what to do on it, how to act, even where to sit.

The idea of leaving his familiar world was overwhelming and terrifying, but there was also excitement about experiencing some-thing new, of actually making progress on the problem which had nagged the brothers for months. The journey would still be difficult and intimidating, but he knew that he needed to take it in order to track down Uncle Barnaby. Or at least try to.

He had never been in a place like San Francisco before, or any big city, for that matter. The small village of Casey's Fork was the largest settlement he had been to. How would he navigate a town three, four, ten times as big? Where would he stay? How would he get around?

His thoughts circled backed to Lily. No matter how he would travel around San Francisco, it wouldn't be on her. He sighed and stroked her neck again. A moment later a clatter of a horse's hoofs on the road behind announced another arrival.

"Allen! Allen! Stop!" came a loud call.

Allen reined in Lily and turned in his saddle. A familiar figure bore down on him.

"Ike Watson! What brings you out here?" Allen said as the old hunter came up next to him.

"Allen, by all the good fortunes of the Rockies!" yelled Ike. "Just the boy I'm pinin' to see. Sighted ye from the ridge."

"And I'm mighty glad to see you, too, Ike," returned the young rancher. "I want a bit of advice, and you are just the man to give it to me."

"Advice? I'm ready to give ye bushels of it, if it will do ye the least bit of good, lad," Ike said. "Why yer headed away from yer ranch? Where are ye going?"

"I'm on my way to the railroad station. I am bound for San Francisco to hunt up Uncle Barnaby," Allen said.

"Gee whiz! Now I call fortunate!" Ike said. "If I hadn't a catched ye, ye would be goin' off on a wild goose chase, with no end to that path."

"A wild goose chase? Why? What do you mean?" Allen leaned toward Ike excitedly. "Ike, did you find out anything about my uncle? Did you get something from him?"

Ike shook his head. "No, I ain't got no word from him, but I got word in a way that two rascals didn't dream on."

"What two rascals? Who are they? What do you know?" asked Allen impatiently.

Ike held up a hand to deflect the barrage of questions. "Not much, to tell the truth, and yet a great deal."

Allen stared at him in puzzlement. "I'm not all aboard."

"Well, I'll tells ye. It happened this mornin', when I was down to Casey's Fork," Ike explained. "I was ridin' along the old Bar Trail when here comes a couple of the worst lookin' bad men ye ever seed. Says one to the other, 'If we can make him tell us where the mine is, we will all become rich.' Then says the other, 'We'll make him speak. We didn't trap him inter leavin' Frisco for nuthin'.' Now, these fellers were on the bottom trail, while I were up on the rocks. I aimed to get to 'em to make 'em tell me what was the meanin' of it all, but they spied me comin' down, and by the grasshoppers of Kansas! ye ought to seed 'em put an' scoot. They got out of sight in a jiffy, and I couldn't locate 'em, try my best. I hung around an hour, and then I made up my mind to ride over and tell ye what I had heard."

"Trapped into leaving San Francisco!" gasped Allen. "They must mean Uncle Barnaby. Who else could it be? Paul, Chet and I reckoned something like that happened. Did they say where they had taken him? What else did they say?"

"Didn't say nuthin' more than I told ye," The hunter from Gold Fork shrugged. "Leastwise, didn't say nothin' I could hear."

"Did you know these men?"

"I don't, exceptin' I seed them hangin' around Jordan Creek about six months ago. Like as not they belong to the old Sol Davids gang," Ike snorted. "Nearly every one up that water course belonged to that bunch at one time or the other."

"Would you recognize them if you saw them again?" Allen pressed.

"Of course!" Ike slapped one of his huge hands on his chest. "I'm powerful good at recollectin' faces once I see 'em."

"Where do you suppose the men went to?" Allen wondered.

"Rode off towards Black Rock River Canyon." Ike nodded in the general direction.

Allen started. Could it be they suspected the claim was up in that neighborhood, so close to the ranch? It was more than possible. He thought for a moment. "Ike, I'm going to change my plans about going to San Francisco. It would certainly appear to be a useless trip now. I am going after those two men!"

"I like that talk, Allen!" cried Ike. "This here state would be a hundred per cent better off with them fellers out of it."

Allen gazed at Ike Watson earnestly. "Will you help me in this work? You understand more about these bad men than I do."

"Will I help ye? Why Allen, ye ought to know better than to ask such a question. Why, ye know the sons of Granville Winthrup are like my own! Of course, I'll help ye. I ain't got much to do. Them new claims up the Salmon can wait well enough."

A discussion followed. Because of the lateness of the hour, they decided to return to the Crossroads Hotel and spend the night. Daddy Wampole was a little surprised to see Allen again so soon, but quickly informed him of Paul's discovery of the paper scraps and his suspicion about Captain Grady.

"Now there is not the slightest doubt but what my uncle was decoyed away from San Francisco," Allen said, pounding the kitchen table with one hand, "lured by some forged letter that maybe Grady had a hand in. For the first time in months, I feel we can learn more about Uncle Barnaby's disappearance. It's more important than ever to find those men, Ike."

"We will," Ike assured him calmly.

Allen turned to Daddy, "When did Paul and Chet head back to the ranch?"

"About two or three hours ago," Daddy replied.

"At least I won't have to worry about them," Allen said. "They can't get into any more trouble there. Where uncle is now is the mystery which those two men must solve for me."

Allen and Ike retired early. Allen had a lot to think about. Things had broken free finally. Events were tumbling now faster, like an avAllenche beginning with a few rocks, growing larger and stronger with each passing moment. He shuddered whenever he thought that his uncle might be in peril of his life. Allen lay awake all night, turning the problem over and over in his mind.

"Those men would indeed dare all for gold, as those initials on the cross imply," Allen muttered to himself. "What a pity they were not exterminated the time old Sol Davids was hanged."

Toward morning Allen slipped into a restless slumber, only to be startled awake by a touch from Ike Watson's hand an hour later.

"Time to climb below and feed up, Allen," said the old hunter. "We have a long ride afore us."

"That's true!" Allen sprang to his feet. At last, he believed he could actually do something about the situation he and his brothers found themselves in.

After a substantial but hasty breakfast, the two saddled their horses and set off. Daddy Wampole sent them off with a waving of his hand and best wishes.

"We'll make for Casey's Fork first off," proposed Ike. "Perhaps I can pick up the trail there. If I can't, we can push on toward the Salmon and trust to luck."

Allen felt unsure if even the old hunter could find the track again after such a long time, but he pushed down his doubt. After all, he didn't have any other plan. Ike's information was the best he had; it might be his only hope. So Allen agreed to Ike's idea.

They reached Casey's Fork, a rough tumble of boulders in a bend of the Umihalo Creek, at noon. Allen was glad enough to dismount and take shade in the shadow of the rocks while Ike went off on a tour of inspection. He was gone so long that Allen at last grew alarmed.

"Something must be wrong, or he would be back before this," Allen said to himself. "Time to go after him."

But he had hardly climbed into the saddle when he heard a shout ahead. Looking beyond a belt of shrubs he saw Ike signaling to him.

"Found it!" he exulted as Allen galloped up. "They took the creek road over to the forest trail. The marks are fresh, showin' they didn't move on until dark last night."

"That means they can't be that far in front of us!" Allen's face set in grim determination. "If we can only keep moving till we catch up to them!"

"No time to lose," said Ike Watson, and once more they continued the pursuit, this time faster than before.

Yet at the end of two miles they came to a sudden halt. The hoof prints led down to the bank of a shallow stream and there disappeared from view.

"Gone!" burst from Allen's lips. His confidence crashed. "What's to do now?"

Ike halted in perplexity for fully a minute. He dismounted and waded into the water, which was scarcely a foot to a foot and a half in depth.

"Ho! Ho! Ho!" he shouted suddenly. "I thought so! No, ye can't play that game here."

"What game, Ike?" questioned Allen, perking up.

"They went up in the middle of this here stream, thinkin' they could throw me off their tail. Look, here are the hoof prints as plain as the nose on yer face." And the old hunter pointed into the clear water.

Letting Allen bring his horse, Watson walked slowly along the bed of the waterway, careful to keep his feet from the sunken holes. His eyes scanned every inch for the crescent-moon marks of horseshoes. After half a mile, at a point where the brush along the bank thinned, a small clearing appeared. The trail emerged once more on the dirt and rocks.

"An old trick, but it didn't work this trip," chuckled Ike to Allen, as he once more resumed his seat in the saddle and the two set off again.

"What I am thinking of is, what made them suspicious, after they were so far from Casey's Forks?" Allen answered his own question sarcastically. "Perhaps their guilty consciences."

"That, an' because they thought I might be follerin' them." Ike said. "Hullo! What does this mean?"

They had followed the tracks around a belt of timber and into a stretch of land with loose rocks. Near the rocks was a recently used camp: a smoldering fire and some odds and ends of crackers and meat.

"We ain't far behind 'em, Allen!" Ike exclaimed. "Somebody tended to this fire less than a couple of hours ago."

"Then let us push on, by all means. If we can reach those two men before they have a chance to join any of their companions, so much the better." Allen eagerly looked up ahead. "The path leads along the rocks. Do you have any idea where we are going?"

"Idea! Why, Allen, this here country is like a book to me," laughed Ike. "Don't ye get afeared of being lost so long as ye stay nigh me."

"I didn't mean that, Ike!" Allen felt his cheeks flush in embarrassment at sounding like he doubted his guide. "I mean, do you think you got where the men went from here?"

Ike sized up the path in front of him. "Up to Grizzly Pass, most likely, an' then along over to the Black Rock Canyon. Eh, Allen?"

Allen nodded. "It would seem so. That would make sense."

Despite the fierce sunshine, it was deliciously cool along the base of the rocky wall, and the horses made progress over the hard but level ground. Here and there immense brier bushes overhung the way, but the animals avoided these, although they seemed more afraid of them than were their riders.

They reached the top of the rocks half an hour later, and they moved back to where the way was smooth and safe. They stopped for a short lunch from their pouches. Allen wasn't particularly hungry, but they had to allow their horses some rest. The meal finished, they went forward as fast as the still fatigued horses would carry them.

"I don't see a trail." Allen shaded his eyes with one hand as he scanned the area.

"There ain't no need to here," responded Ike Watson. "This here way is a blind pocket for all these three miles or so. Ye couldn't go no different if ye tried. By-and-by, when we come out on Sampson's Flats, we'll look for the trail again."

"We ought to catch up to those men before we reach the flats," observed Allen hopefully. "They must be wore out by that climb."

"We ain't far off," reassured Watson. "Just keep silent half an hour longer, and we'll—"

He broke off short, reigned in his steed, and pointed ahead.

Allen's and Ike's attention focused on a lone pine tree. Under its branches, two men slept against the tree's trunk. Their horses were hobbled only a few feet away. Neither man seemed to know that Allen and Ike were approaching, judging from the peaceful look on their faces. Both men held smoking pipes in their mouths.

"Is that them?" Allen whispered.

Ike nodded.

"Let us dismount and sneak our way to them," suggested Allen in a quiet voice. "If we secure their horses first, they will have no chance to get away from us."

"Ace-high idea, lad," said Watson, in an equally low tone.

Sliding to the ground, they led their horses behind some heavy brush and secured the reins to some branches. With weapons at the ready, Allen and Ike crept up behind to where the mounts belonging to the two bad men from Jordan Creek grazed.

Allen and the old hunter went about their work as silently as bobcats on the prowl. The horses stood somewhat behind the dozing men, and so Allen and Ike made a detour, coming up behind their quarry like twin shadows.

Allen led the animals back to his horse and tethered them there. The first task was complete; now he returned to Ike, still standing guard with his trusty gun aimed and ready, in case of trouble.

"Now, what's to do?" Allen whispered.

"Maybe we had better git a few ropes ready, in case we want to bind 'em," began Ike, but before this idea could be put into execution, one of the men's pipes slipped out of his mouth, and the hot tobacco, falling on his hand, brought him upright with a start. He opened his eyes, and with a loud exclamation, spotted Allen and Ike. This awoke his companion, who leaped to his feet.

"What does this mea—" began the second man.

"Hands up, ye rascals!" barked Ike, so sternly that instantly both arms of the man were raised high overhead.

The second man, in his sitting position, made a reach to draw his pistol. Allen fired, his bullet ricocheting off the tree trunk. Startled, the man fumbled his gun, dropped it to the dirt, then put up his hands.

"We have ye, strangers," remarked Ike after a second of silence. "Do ye acknowledge the corn?"

"What's the meaning of this outrage?" demanded the fellow who was standing, as he scowled fiercely, first at Ike and then Allen.

"It means firstly that ye are in our power," grinned Ike. It was evident that he thoroughly enjoyed the affair.

"Well?" asked the standing man.

"Then ye acknowledge that, do ye?" Ike insisted.

"I guess we'll have to," the standing man grudgingly replied.

"It's Ike Watson from Gold Fork," put in the man who was sitting.

"Ike Watson!" The face of the speaker grew quite disturbed. It was plain he recognized Watson's name and did not relish being held up by the well-known old man.

"Ye-as, I'm Ike Watson," drawled the old hunter. "Now, give me yer handles, and let me have 'em straight."

"My name is Roe Bluckburn," came from the standing man.

"Mine is Lou Slavin, and I'm not ashamed of it," said the other.

"Just so," mused Watson. "I've heared both of you belongin' to the old Sol Davids gang of horse thieves."

"You're wrong. We aren't outlaws of any sort," blustered Bluckburn, who appeared the leader of the pair.

"Well, we won't quarrel about that, seein' as how we are on another path today," Ike went on. "We want ye to up and tell us about a missing man."

"Yes, and tell us honest," put in Allen, grimly.

The men were both taken aback by the request. They exchanged glances and each waited for the other to speak.

"Come, out with it, Bluckburn!" ordered Ike.

Bluckburn shrugged. "Dunno the man you're talking about."

"Ye can't come it that way. Didn't I hear ye talkin' it over down to Casey's Forks only yesterday? Come, out with the truth, or take the consequences!" Ike tapped his Colt's barrel.

Bluckburn gulped, but recovered his composure. "Must be some mistake. We ain't been near Casey's Fork in, what, a month. Eh, Lou?"

"Nixy." Slavin shrugged.

"Ye tell it so smooth I would most believe ye, if I didn't followed ye up," growled Ike.

"Listen, we don't know nothing about no Barnaby Winthrup," Slavin angrily sputtered.

"How did you know we were asking about Barnaby Winthrup?" Allen jumped in. "We said we were after a missing man. Neither one of us mentioned that name. Did we, Ike?"

Ike shook his head. "That's right. But now we found out ye are in the deal against Barnaby Winthrup, and I am helping his nephew here, Allen Winthrup. So ye had better ease yer mind at once. Understand?"

The two men turned their gaze to Allen curiously.

"Are ye fellers goin' to speak?" roared Ike. "Ye can't expect me to stand here with a gun the rest of the day!"

"Unless you do talk, we'll hand you over to the sheriff. We believe we have a good case against you," said Allen. He remembered the information Daddy Wampole had told him, and a thought popped into his mind. He added, "And we will have a better one after Captain Grady is placed under arrest."

"Captain Grady!" groaned the man named Lou Slavin. "I reckon the jig is up, Roe."

"Shut up!" snarled Bluckburn.

"But if the captain is known what show have we got?" grumbled Slavin. He continued anxiously. "Say? I went into this thing against my will, an' I wish I was out of it. Supposin' I tell yer everything about the whole gang, does that save me?"

"Don't you say nothin', Lou!" threatened Bluckburn, but before he could speak further the cocking of Ike's gun caused him to retreat back to the tree, where he stood, not daring to say another word.

"Go on and have yer say!" commanded the old hunter to Lou Slavin. "And, as I said before, give it to us straight. Where is Barnaby Winthrup?"

"He is a prisoner, about ten miles from here," came Slavin's flat and sudden reply.

Chapter 11

P aul filled with anger, but he caged the beast, as he glared at Captain Grady. "What does this mean?"

"Reckon you have eyes an' can see," scoffed Captain Grady. "I told you that you hadn't seen the end of this, an' that I would have this place in my possession pretty quick."

"You had no right to break into our house and fire our things out!" Chet shouted.

"I deny as how this is your house, youngster. It belongs to me, as does the whole ranch property. A young savage told me once that possession is nine parts of the law, an' now the possession is mine," Grady smirked. "The faster you two get off my ground the better it will suit me."

"We won't move an inch until we put our things back into that house," retorted Chet as he advanced with Rush.

"Halt where you are!" Captain Grady raised his gun and aimed it at Chet. "You'll not come near this porch, mind that!"

"I'm going in, and you won't stop me," declared Chet. "And you're gonna answer—"

Paul didn't want Chet to warn Grady know they suspected him of anything. He rode up to his younger brother and plucked him by the sleeve. "Wait, Chet. Don't be rash."

"Smart thinkin' for a young savage. Either of you two try to cross this gateway and I'll fire on you, sure as fate," the captain went on.

Urged by Paul, Chet brought Rush to a stand. The boys were about thirty feet from where Captain Grady stood on guard.

"Now, the best thing you fellers can do," said the captain, sharply, "is to ride over to Dottery's ranch, an' get a wagon an' tote these things away. If they are left more 'n a week, I'll pitch them into the river, mind you."

"What about our livestock?" Chet challenged.

"Ain't yours anymore, monkey," Grady said. Again the man smiled sarcastically. "If you ain't satisfied at the way matters have turned, you can go to law, just as you advised me to do."

"We certainly will go to law," asserted Paul. "Are you alone here?"

"That's not for you to ask," rebuffed Grady.

"I assume you hung around here and saw Allen and I go off," Paul said.

"I ain't standing here as a target for questions," growled Grady.

"You are a sneak and worse, Captain Grady!" burst out Chet. "If law exists in this state, you will receive your full dose of it, mark my word!"

"Ha! You young monkey, don't talk to me in that fashion," thundered the Captain in a rage. "Come, I've told you what is best to do. Now clear out. I shall keep an eye out, an' if you attempt to play any trick in the dark on me you'll find yourself running up against a charge of buckshot."

It was very evident that Captain Grady spoke in dead earnest. His forehead crinkled and his eyes squinted as he looked the brothers in the eye. He scowled viciously and walked a step forward.

Yet the brothers were not daunted. They held their ground, and Paul even took a slight move ahead on Jasper's back.

"Supposing we go to Mr. Dottery's place," said Paul. "If we tell our story, don't you imagine he will turn in and help us bounce you out of here?"

"No, you'll find no help at Dottery's," Grady fired back.

"He is our friend, and he will not stand for your doings, even if you do own the ranch over the river," Paul challenged.

"Well then, why don't you jest go an' see your pal Dottery and find out," snapped Captain Grady.

"We will—and some other people, too," Chet added.

"And in the meantime, if any of our belongings are damaged, you'll pay for it," Paul pledged.

"I won't be responsible for anything! Now clear out an' leave me alone." Grady waved his gun to emphasize his order.

With a nod, both Paul and Chet turned their horses and rode down the river trail to the stand of cottonwoods. They had a lot to think about and no idea of what to do next.

"It's a shame, Paul!" Chet spat out, almost crying with rage. "We ought to have shot him where he stood."

"I suppose many a man would have done it," Paul spoke somewhat moodily, "but he didn't this by himself."

"How do you mean?"

"He didn't answer when I asked if he was alone. Grady didn't tote all our belongings outside by himself. He probably had help," Paul said. "Whoever that was could have been hidden in the shadows. If we made a wrong move against the so-called captain, they could have dropped us."

"I never thought of that," Chet admitted.

"Nevertheless, we must remove him." Paul spoke with grim determination.

"He won't go out without a fight."

"I think he will—when we round up enough of a crowd against him," Paul reasoned.

"He must have been hanging around, watching for his chance, like you said," went on Chet. "Who knows but what he, or one of his men, may have been spying on us ever since his last visit."

"I hope not, Chet," Paul said. "That could mean he overheard us talking about Uncle Barnaby's gold mine."

"You're right!" Chet groaned out. "What if he did? He is scoundrel enough to try to locate it and set up a claim, eh?"

"Undoubtedly," Paul confirmed. "Come on. The best we can do is to go to Mr. Dottery's and attempt to get aid. We have a long journey by night, but there's nothing else we can do."

"I won't mind it—if only Mr. Dottery will turn in and help us," Chet said. "He ought to, but he was always a peculiar fellow. He may not want to make an enemy of Captain Grady, seeing as their ranches adjoin. But let's go, while daylight lasts. There's not much left."

The two brothers headed out along the river trail. They could see the golden orb of the sun dwindle in size, fading behind the distant line of mountain peaks. The air cooled as they urged their horses on. Paul and Chet knew the way well, having traveled it a dozen times in search of stray cattle. The brothers rode side by side, not talking at all. Bit by bit the sun faded from view behind the distant mountains, casting long shadows over the level stretches and the foothills beyond. The night birds sang their parting song, and then came the almost utter silence of the night. They continued to ride, urging on their weary horses.

"When do you suppose we'll reach Mr. Dottery's?" questioned Chet, after several miles had been covered.

"If all goes well, we'll be there by eleven or twelve o'clock," estimated his brother, "and remember we need to go across Demon Hollow, not a fool of a job in the dark, even with some moon."

"Especially if the demon is abroad," laughed Chet nervously.

In the darkness the steady rhythm of their horse's hoof beats sounded out doubly loud on the hard-packed road, but that was better than the intense stillness of before.

"I feel a hundred miles from nowhere at all," commented Paul uneasily.

Their mounts were so tired that the boys had their hands full making them keep their gait. They would trot a few steps and then drop into a stolid walk.

"I don't blame them much. They're doing two days' work in one. But never mind," Chet patted Rush's neck, "they've earned a rest soon."

By ten o'clock it was pitch dark. To be sure the stars were shining, but they gave only a feeble light. The brothers had to hold their animals at a tight rein to keep them from stumbling into unexpected holes.

"It will be nearer one than midnight before we end up there at this rate," grumbled Paul. "Just look ahead and see how dark and forbidding the Hollow looks."

"Not the most cheerful spot in the world by day, let alone night," rejoined Chet, as he strained his eyes to pierce the heavy shadows. "Let's move through it as fast as we can."

"Afraid, Chet?" Paul chided. "You don't believe in the old trappers' stories about the ghost in hiding at the bottom of the rocky pass, do you?"

"Oh, no, no...only I...I would rather be on the flat trail beyond here," Chet said.

Paul said no more, having no desire to hurt his little brother's feelings. To tell the exact truth, he felt a bit uneasy as the time grew toward midnight.

Down and down the road ran, between two rocky crags. Soon the brothers had to let the horses pick their own way as best they might. The rocky ground slipped away at times beneath the horses' hooves, dislodging stones from time to time with a startling loudness. To either side, the looming boulders stretched upward, as though they might tumble at any moment and crush the travelers beneath an avalanche of rock.

Suddenly Chet gave a start and a cry. "Paul, what is that?"

"Where?"

"Over to the left!"

Paul turned in his saddle. As he did so an object not over two feet long and of a gray and white color, with some black, swept to one side of them.

"Can it be the demon?" gasped Chet.

Paul laughed. "Your demon is just a badger, out on the forage. Don't you smell him?"

"Oh." Chet chuckled to cover his embarrassment. He recovered and readied his rifle. He tried to take aim in the gloom.

"Don't fire!" Paul said. "What is the use? Don't a waste the ammunition. It isn't hurting anything, and he's a good distance from the ranch. Let him go."

By the time Chet had listened to all this and lowered his rifle, the badger had disappeared. The animal was not used to being disturbed and was most likely more frightened than Chet.

They passed on until they reached the very bottom of the Hollow. The horses slowly continued, as if knowing the place was perilous. Rush stumbled down into a hole, almost throwing Chet over his head. Chet held on, and Rush arose all right. A small smudge of blood was on his left foreleg.

The two peered with watchful eyes up and down the silent pass. A pall of silence hung heavily over the area, which was as empty and black as a crow's eye. The narrow strip between the two walls was bare except for some water that trickled along one side, flowing through in a small brook alongside the trail with a muffled murmur. The wind sighed through the deep opening, and that was all. It reminded Paul of his experience in the caverns, and he shuddered. In another five minutes the pass would be behind them.

Both boys drew a long breath of relief when they reached the high ground beyond at last. The moon began to rise. The tension left the brothers, and now, by contrast, the road looked to them as bright as if awash in sunlight.

"Come to think of it, we might as well take it easy," remarked Paul. "It isn't likely that Mr. Dottery will want to make a move before morning."

"Yes, but if we reach his place sooner, it will give us a chance to rest up a bit. We need that, and so do the horses," Chet suggested.

"I didn't think of that. You're right, Chet. Well, forward we go."

An hour passed and then another, after which Chet gave a joyous cry. "Look! Dottery's outbuildings! We'll soon be there now!"

"Right you are, Chet. I wonder—" Paul stopped short. "Wait, look over there!"

He pointed to a barn not a great distance back from the road. The door of the structure was open and the light of a lantern flashed inside.

"Dottery must be up, or else—" began Chet.

The brothers spoke the words simultaneously. "Horse thieves!"

Chapter 12

C ould it be possible that the gang were raiding their nearest neighbor? Chet started to turn Rush toward the barn.

"Wait! Don't do anything impulsive! Let's dismount and investigate," cautioned Paul in a whisper.

The two slid off their saddles, securing Rush and Jasper behind some brush. Guns in hand, they crept across the road and over a wire fence into the field. They knelt behind the thick grass and weeds. Three men came out of the barn, leading four horses. The horses' heads bobbed up and down as the outlaws led them through an opening in the fence not fifteen feet from where the boys lay.

Chet put his lips next to Paul's ear and spoke almost inaudibly. "The two in front ... they were the ones I tangled with on the trail. The first one's called Saul, and the second hombre's handle is Darry. Don't recognize the third."

The horse thieves move toward any opening in the fence. Chet drew up his pistol and pointed it at the leader.

"Don't fire! Wait!" Paul hissed as he pushed Chet's gun hand down. "There are three of them, remember."

"I wonder where Mr. Dottery is?"

"Asleep, most likely," Paul responded.

"We ought to rouse him," said Chet. "Run, Paul, while I keep them in sight."

"I will, but don't do anything foolish. Just keep an eye on them," said Paul.

Paul waited until Chet nodded, then sneaked along in the tall grass until he reached the last outbuilding. He sped like a deer across a hundred feet toward the ranch home, showing dimly in the inky shadows ahead.

Less than sixty seconds passed, and he was rapping vigorously on the front door of the heavy log building, glancing over his shoulder toward the barn, hoping the sound wouldn't carry to the others. Not content with using his fist, he kicked with the toe of his cowhide boot.

"Who's thar?" came a groggy voice from within.

"Mr. Dottery!" Paul called quietly.

"That's me, stranger."

"It's Paul Winthrup. Come out. There are horse thieves at your barn."

"What!" bellowed Dottery. He unbarred the door and came out on a run, gun in hand and a long pistol in his belt. He was a heavy-built man, with a voice like a giant. An old settler, he rarely bothered to undress when he went to rest for the night. "The same chaps that robbed you?"

"Yes, the same, unless I'm very much mistaken," Paul said. "My brother Chet is watching them now."

"I'll fix 'em. Go back and call my hired hand, Jack." Dottery pointed to the small nearby bunkhouse.

Paul did as directed. It took some time to wake the cowboy, Jack Blowfen, but once roused, the man quickly took in the situation, and arming himself, joined in a rush after Dottery, followed by Paul.

"The lousy bandits!" the hired hand muttered. "Yer brother told us about 'em when he stopped here on his way to the railroad station. Too bad Ike Watson didn't plug every one of 'em when he had the chance. Next thing yer know they'll be runnin' off with a bunch o' the herd."

"Be careful when you shoot. Chet is near them," said Paul, "I don't want him to be taken for a horse thief in the dark."

"I know the lad, and I also know this Saul Mangle and his gang," Blowfen said. "I owe Mangle one for the way he treated me in Deadwood one day."

He ran so swiftly that Paul worked hard to keep up with him, but he stumbled over the unfamiliar ground. Blowfen reached the top of the hill before Paul crested it, but he sprinted away into the night, leaving Paul behind. He was out of sight before Paul could catch his breath and run after the hired hand.

Bang! Bang! The shots came from behind the barn, while Paul was some distance away.

"Paul! Paul! Hold on!"

It was Chet's voice. As he cried out, he jumped to his feet and grabbed his brother by the sleeve. Paul had almost stepped on him.

"Come on, Chet," Paul tilted his head toward the sound of the gunshots.

"I'm coming. But shouldn't we better look to our horses?"

"In a minute. Let's find out what that firing means." Paul drew his revolver.

Paul led the way toward the barn. There, in the furtive light that filtered through cracks in the worn boards, they saw two men struggling violently: Dottery and the third man. Mangle, Nodley and Blowfen were nowhere to be seen. Two horses were running about wildly, alarmed by the shots in the dark. Both wore bridles but had no saddles.

"Catch the hosses!" commanded Dottery, as he made out the forms of the boys. "Don't let 'em get out of that break in the fence!"

"Have you that man?" Paul called out.

"I will have in a second."

The brothers holstered their guns and rushed for the animals. It was no light work to secure them. When they accomplished that, they ran the horses into the barn and closed the doors. As they walked out of the barn, their hearts still pounding, they heard a gunshot from the brush on the opposite side of the road, and then the voice of Blowfen calling out:

"Let them hosses go, you rascals! Take that, Saul Mangle, fer the trick yer played me in Deadwood!"

"Rush and Jasper!" Chet said to Paul. "Those owlhoots aren't going to steal them a second time!"

He darted in the direction of the encounter, with Paul on his heels. The wire fence seemed to part at a single bound and they dove into the brush pell-mell. Off to their left, they could hear two men thrashing around at a lively rate, so Blowfen was probably having a fierce hand-to-hand contest with his antagonist.

"You've hit me in the leg, and I'll never forgive you for it!" Saul Mangle exclaimed. "How do you like that, you milk-and-water cow puncher?"

"I don't like it, and ain't going ter stand it, yer low down hoss robber and gambler," returned Blowfen, and then came the fall of one body over another, just as Paul and Chet leaped into the little opening where the battle was taking place.

Blowfen lay on his back with Saul Mangle on top of him. The horse thief had the butt of a heavy pistol raised threateningly. He spun around in surprise at the appearance of Paul and Chet.

"Let up there!" ordered Paul. "Let up at once!"

The cry and the sight of the boys' weapons decided Mangle. With a muttering he gave Blowfen's body a kick and sprang for the bushes. Chet and Paul plunged after him, leaving the cowboy to stagger to his feet and regain his pistols. The brothers raced through the brush. They had nearly caught up with Mangle when they ran into Darry, who held several horses, including Jasper and Rush. He must have been waiting for the head of the outlaws to finish his quarrel with Blowfen.

As Mangle ducked under a branch and reached for the closest of the animals, Paul grabbed him by the shoulder. The boy wrenched Mangle's gun out of his hand and threw it away.

"Stop!" he called. "You cannot take those horses. We will shoot you both if you attempt it!"

Darry swore and attempted to move on, thinking Mangle would follow. But now Chet barred the way.

The ranch boy had his revolver up and there was a determined look on his sunburned face. He appeared to be fighting for Rush as much as for anything else.

"Off that horse!" was all he said, but the tone in which the words left no room for argument.

Darry hesitated and reached at first to feel for his own weapon, but then he changed his mind. Blowfen came through the bushes.

"We'll have to make tracks," Darry yelled to Mangle, and leaped to the ground, putting the horse between himself and Chet, and scrambled for cover.

Mangle swung around and struck Paul with a solid right cross. Paul released his grip and reeled backward. Chet ran up to Paul.

"Where are they?" roared Blowfen, running up. "Which way did they go?"

Paul pointed to where the two had fled. At once Blowfen took off in pursuit. In another second Chet and Paul were alone with the horses. The sounds from the distance told them that Mangle and Nodley were doing their best to escape from the neighborhood.

"Our money!" uttered Chet in despair. "We ought to have made an effort to get our savings back!"

"True, but it's too late now, barring we go after the pair on horseback." Paul rubbed his sore chin and worked his jaw side to side.

"Let's return Mr. Dottery's horses to the barn first and see how he has made out with the other man."

They took the horses in charge, passed with them across the road and through the break in the wire fence. At the barn they found the ranch owner in the act of making the last thief a prisoner by tying his hands and legs with odd bits of harness straps.

"Got this one, anyway," crowed Dottery. "Whar are the others?"

"Jack Blowfen has gone after them," Paul gestured toward the animals. "Here are your horses."

"Good enough. Say, will you guard this man if I go after Jack?" Dottery went on, anxiously.

"Of course," urged Chet. "If you can capture Saul Mangle, do so. We believe he has seven hundred dollars belonging to us."

"So Allen told me," Dottery said as he made for his livestock.

The boys took charge of the prisoner, and mounting one of his animals, Dottery rode out of the enclosure. He took the lantern with him, leaving those behind in darkness.

"Strike a light, Chet, and see if you can't find another lamp in the barn," said Paul. "I'll make sure this guy doesn't get away."

"This is hard on a poor man," moaned the thief.

"Maybe you ought to have thought of that before you started in this business," Paul noted dryly. "You know full well how stern the justice usually is handed out to horse thieves in this section of the country."

"It was Mangle coaxed me into the work. He said as how he had a right to the horses. Said he won them in a poker game," the bound man claimed.

"Indeed! I suppose he said he had a right to our horses, too," Paul said, with a sarcasm that was entirely lost on the prisoner.

"Yes, he did."

"In that case you will suffer for your simpleness."

Chet came back to Paul. "No lantern in the barn, so far as I can see."

"We'd better march this guy up to the house," Paul said.

"He can't march with his legs tied," Chet observed with a grin.

Paul returned the smile. "No, but I reckon he can hobble a bit."

Chet and Paul each caught the man by the arm, and groaning and muttering, pulled him toward the ranch home like a scarecrow being taken to a corn field. After arriving at Dottery's cabin, Paul noticed their prisoner had received an ugly injury in the shoulder.

"Chet, make sure all the horses are back in the barn and lock the door, so that they're safe, at least for the time being," Paul said, "I'll tend to … what is your name?"

"Jeff Jones," answered the man.

"I'll take care of Jones' wound," Paul finished.

"Will you be all right by yourself with him?" Chet nodded toward Jones.

"I should be," Paul looked at the prisoner. "He's trussed up pretty good."

Paul rummaged around in the kitchen until he found supplies that he would need to clean and bandage his captive's injury. He set the supplies next to Jones and opened the man's shirt, then he cleaned and bandaged the wound. He was careful not to hurt Jones but tried to do as much as he could. Paul also took good care, however, that the captive should be allowed any chance of freedom.

"What are you goin' to do with me?" asked Jones as the work progressed. "Ain't goin' to tote me to town, are you?"

"That depends upon what Mr. Dottery says," replied Paul. "He's the boss of this ranch."

"Better let me go," threatened the man, "If you don't there will be big trouble ahead."

"Don't imagine we are to be scared so easily," Paul brushed off.

"We have a bigger rascal to deal with even than you," Chet put in as he came back into the room.

"You mean Saul Mangle?" asked Jones.

"No, I'm talking about a much larger snake: Captain Hank Grady," said Chet.

"Captain Hank Grady! What do you know of him?" Jones sounded shocked. "Did you know about him and your Uncle Barnaby—" The man broke off short.

"My Uncle Barnaby!" cried Chet. "What made you think of him in connection with Captain Grady?"

Jones' expression was like a bad poker player who just drew the winning card. "Oh, I know a lot about him and the captain. A heap that maybe you boys would give a lot to know about."

Chapter 13

"**M**y uncle is a prisoner about ten miles from here?" repeated a stunned Allen after Lou Slavin made his surprising statement.

"Will you shut yer mouth?" howled Bluckburn savagely to his confederate. "You'll spoil everything."

He made a threatening move toward Slavin. Ike checked the advance with a wave of his gun.

"An' he'll spare hisself from bein' lynched," added Ike. "Besides, I'm kinda interested in what he's sayin'."

"As am I," put in Allen.

"We haven't done anything. You can't hold us," spluttered Bluckburn. He seemed to understand he found himself in a bad corner.

"I presume you believe holding a man a prisoner against his will is 'nothing.' I believe that is called kidnapping," Allen's voice dripped with sarcasm. He turned his attention back to the first man. "Go on. Where is my uncle? Let's have the whole story."

Slavin blurted out a full confession, telling how Bluckburn had followed Uncle Barnaby to San Francisco. He wanted to learn the secret of a new claim, which Bluckburn realized must be valuable. The outlaw went on, blaming the other man for sending a forged letter to Allen's uncle, calling the old prospector back to his home, as well as the one canceling the meeting with the investor. Afterwards, Bluckburn sent word by telegraph to the other members of the thieving band, and when Barnaby Winthrup got off at the nearest railroad station to the ranch, he was trailed and waylaid.

"The crowd had a mighty hard time with him, he fought so," said Slavin.

"Good for Uncle Barnaby," Allen cheered.

"Once he nearly got away, but Captain Grady tripped him up an' then he was bound tight," Slavin said.

"Captain Grady!" Allen spat out the name with disgust. "My hunch was right. He has his hands all over this."

"About his size," returned Ike. "I always allowed as how he was one o' the shady class."

"He... he's the head of the whole business," put in Slavin eagerly. He apparently began to think it time to try to clear himself. "I only acted under his say so."

"It's too late fer ye ter open yer mouth," Ike cut him short.

"No, Ike, no. If this man helps us, I'll see what I can do for him," Allen offered.

"As ye say, Allen," Ike grumbled. "Keep talkin', Slavin. Where's Barnaby Winthrup? Straight, now, remember. No corral dust."

"He's held in a cave," Slavin told them, "I don't know the lay o' the land exactly, but I'm comin' purty nigh nearby."

"Would you know the spot if you were in the area?" asked Allen.

"I think I would." The thief nodded, casting an uncomfortable look toward the glowering Bluckburn.

"We must take him along," the young ranchman proposed to Ike, "but what shall we do with Bluckburn?"

"He ought ter be lynched now," came the old hunter's stern reply. "During my days trappin' in the mountains, we had no use for jails and lockups. We fixed up things right there and then."

"We'll let the law attend to Bluckburn, Ike," Allen said.

"Twernt they the part of the same gang tryin' to lynch ye when I came upon ye?" Ike demanded. "Ye were swingin', as I recollect."

"I recall that, but my Pa never held with lynching," Allen stated firmly. "Neither do I."

"Well, ye are yer Granville's son, that be sure," Ike said with a chuckle after a pause. "All right, no lynchin'. Then what?"

Allen thought for a moment. "Let's take Bluckburn back to Daddy Wampole's place. We'll leave him as a prisoner, and take Slavin along with us, to guide us to where Uncle Barnaby is held."

Ike and Allen secured Bluckburn in his saddle, his feet tied to the stirrups and hands tied to the saddle horn. The two also disarmed Slavin, and within half an hour were on their way back to the Crossroads. The ride was a long and tedious for Allen, his patience growing short but he did not have a choice.

Daddy Wampole was just as surprised as he could be to see Allen and Ike walk up with their prisoner. He listened to the tale Allen and Ike told.

"Why, sure, I'll keep him under guard," he said at the conclusion, nodding toward Bluckburn. "I have a comfy spot in the cellar. An' take my word on it, he shan't escape."

"And in not too long we will add Captain Grady, too," said Allen. "That will give Bluckburn some company."

"It's all Captain Grady's fault! He's to blame!" Bluckburn insisted. "Like Slavin said, we only took orders! Me and him!"

"That be a real tear squeezer," Ike drawled.

"Thank you, Daddy, for watching over Bluckburn." Allen ignored Bluckburn. He turned to Ike and Slavin. "Let's go."

On their way back to the horses, Slavin showed himself more than willing now to do everything and say anything to redeem himself, his reputation, and his neck. Allen still didn't believe Slavin's story enough to arm him, despite the outlaw's repeated requests.

"You just keep ahead, and if any trouble shows itself, we'll keep an eye out for you," Allen directed to Slavin. "This is going to be a long and tough journey before us, likely to try our patience. But we'll have to make do. I don't care what we have to put up with so long as we find my uncle safe and sound."

"That's the talk," answered Ike. "Can't expect ter have every comfort out in these here parts nohow."

The three set out, Slavin in front. The sun, which had been shining brightly all day, grew dark, as cloud after cloud passed over it. Soon the sun was completely covered, casting the landscape into a gray flatness.

"I think we are close to a storm," observed Allen as he surveyed the sky anxiously.

"Seems so," came from Watson. "An' I allow as how it will be a purty heavy one when it comes."

"We've had storms enough lately," said Allen. "I want no more of them."

They continued on their way as rapidly as the ground permitted. Every so often Slavin complained at being pushed on so fast but Watson soon put a stop to his mutterings.

"No use to grumble, Slavin," he said. "Ye can be thankful that we didn't shoot ye down like a dog."

"But I'm not feelin' well," pleaded the evil doer.

"Ain't ye? Well, what ye want is a little exercise," was Watson's sarcastic rejoinder. "So trot ahead, an' let's have no more parley."

Slavin went along, but with a face that looked far from pleasant.

The rain came. When it first splattered against Allen's face, it stung his skin. The drops fell fast and hard, making a drumming noise as they splashed into the puddles on the ground. The air was cold and made one and another of the little party shiver.

"I must say I don't like this," said Allen when he was more than half soaked through. "I wonder if we can't find some shelter until the worst of this is over?"

"Might be as how's there's a cave around," said Watson. "Anyway, we'll keep our eyes peeled fer one."

This they did and a quarter of a mile further on came to something of a cliff overlooking a rocky valley. At the base of the rocky face were a number of rough openings and one of these led to a decent-sized cavern.

"Just the ticket!" cried Watson, as he dismounted and went in the fissure. "We can stay here all night an' by that time the storm will be a thing o' the past. We ain't none too soon either."

Ike was right, for scarcely had they all entered the cavern than the leaden sky let down in all its fury. The rain obscured the landscape, and all became darker than ever.

"Ye set down on that rock," Ike told Slavin. "An' don't ye dare to stir if ye know when yer well off."

"I ain't stirrin'," growled the prisoner.

"I think we had better make a fire," suggested Allen, after the horses had been tied up in a place that was comparatively dry.

"Right ye air, Allen," agreed Watson. "Pervidin' we can find some wood."

"Here is a branch." Allen pointed to a corner of the cavern. "But we may have some difficulty in cutting it up."

"Ho! Ho!" laughed Watson. "Why, Allen, I thought ye were strong lad! We'll bust that up in a jiffy; eh, Slavin?"

"What do ye want?" groused the prisoner.

"Want ye to help break up some firewood."

"Me?"

"Persackly, Slavin. Reckon as how ye want to get as warm as anybody," Ike rubbed his hands together. "Well, ye can start in by doin' some work."

Slavin objected but to no use. He and Ike worked to take branches from the limb, while Allen stacked the pieces for a fire.

"Ike, you are strong," said Allen in open admiration. "I'd give a good lot for your muscles."

"Ye aint' got bad ones yerself, Allen, but ye get stronger when ye stay out here long enough," commented Watson, "The fresh mountain air does it."

"Oh, come, Ike, you know you are extra strong." Allen got as close to joshing as he usually got. "Why, you can do some wonderful things when you want to." To this Watson didn't answer, but the grin on his face displayed that he appreciated the compliment.

The trio soon sat by a crackling fire that seemed to add a glow to the rough cave walls. They drew closer to enjoy the warmth and fixed a meal. They questioned the prisoner about the trail and he said he was certain he was on the right path. Although they were happy with his answers, they were not satisfied; they wanted more from him, but he refused to say anything additional. After they ate, Allen and Watson went near the entrance to the cave, where they huddled close together to discuss their situation. Slavin wished to join them but Allen ordered him back.

"You go back to the fire," he said. "If you want to go to sleep, you may do so."

"Don't trust me even yet, do ye?" muttered the prisoner.

"I do not," Allen bluntly replied.

"Ye're rather hard on a chap what is trying ter do ye a good turn," whined Slavin.

"It remains to be seen if it is a good turn or not. You may be putting up a job on us," Allen said.

"No, I swear everything is on the up and up, Winthrup. Ye'll find everything jest as I told ye."

"Perhaps, but you go back to the fire," Allen commanded.

Slavin returned to the campfire, but his face was dark, as black as the clouds that filled the sky. The prisoner soon lay down and closed his eyes.

"He's still angling for a better deal. He's holding the reins, and knows it," Allen admitted quietly to Ike. "Just dribbling out enough information to keep us hooked. But he did tell us that he thought only a woman had been left in charge of the cave. A woman who claimed to be Darry Nodley's wife."

"Didn't know as how that rascal had one," Ike sounded astonished.

"Well, that is what Slavin said," Allen shrugged

"That might be the truth, and then ag'in, it might not. We don't want to believe too much, Allen," Ike cautioned.

"I agree with you, Ike, but I'm so frustrated," Allen sighed.

The old hunter clamped a reassuring big hand on Allen's shoulder. "Perhaps, but I've seen too much foul play in my time to trust everybody. There may be a woman up there, an' there likely be some men folks too."

Ike went back to the fire. Allen stared out at the storm, anxious to pick up the track to his uncle's prison.

"I wish this rain would stop." He turned away from the mouth of the cave and started to pace.

"I declare, ye getting' as antsy as Chet," Ike grinned. "Wearin' a rut in the ground ain't going dry things up any sooner,"

"I know." Allen sat, but nervous energy almost immediately popped back on his feet again. He picked up a torch from the camp fire. "I'm going to look around."

"Watch out," Ike warned.

"I will." Allen turned toward the back of the cave.

The cavern proved to be a narrow, jagged affair, a hollow split in the rock shaped like a maw of stone. The floor was rough and slid into the back of the cave, rising in a series of uneven steps. Allen climbed the rocks until he had gained a position fifty feet above the entrance. The drop was dizzying.

At a great distance the sound of an underground river reached him, as the rain swept over some boulders at perhaps a rear opening to the cave. Curious to see where the cavern ended, Allen kept climbing until he had left the light of the fire far behind. His torch was burning low, but he whirled it into a blaze and went on once more.

Occasionally he slipped, for the rocks were now wet, but that didn't matter to him. At last, he reached a spot where rain poured in from an out-of-reach opening over his head, forming a miniature waterfall. The water pooled in a small lake.

"This must be a pretty place in the brighter light," he mused. Suddenly, more than the usual amount of water sloshed down, and some splashed over the torch, extinguishing the flame instantly.

Allen frowned and felt in his pocket for his matches. "Confound the luck," he murmured while he hunted for the box. He heard a strange noise overhead, like a scrambling of feet, near the waterfall. Allen listened and the snarl of a wild beast reached his ears.

Allen found and lit a match. He discovered the source of the sound: a wolverine had strayed too near to the opening and had lost its footing on the stone and dropped to a shelf below. The furious creature clawed at the rock in a desperate attempt to find a grip, but its feet skidded on smooth stone. The animal clung on for several seconds, then tumbled again and landed at Allen's feet!

A wolverine was the size of a medium-size dog, around four feet long. The short, muscular legs ended in pads like a cat's that would have allowed him to travel well through a forest floor. As soon as the wolverine smelled the presence of a human being his lips narrowed and his eyes darted quickly to every side, as if to determine how to attack long before he sprang. Even in the feeble light of the match, the glint gave the wolverine's eyes a momentary red glow.

Transferring the match to his left hand, Allen reached for his pistol and brought forth the weapon as swiftly as he could. Without thought or hesitation, the wolverine jumped at Allen with a muffled growl.

Bang! The bullet sliced through the wolverine's right ear and buried itself in the wall behind him. The fierce animal managed almost to make it to Allen's shoulder, but he made a quick twist and freed himself from attack.

His second shot caught the wolverine in the side but did not slow it down at all. With blazing eyes and gleaming teeth, it crouched down and prepared to spring for Allen's throat. He squeezed off another shot just as the match went out and wolverine jumped.

The third report echoed throughout the blackness of the cavern as loudly as had the others, and the crack as the bullet ricocheted off a rock struck fear into Allen's heart. Instinctively, he raised his arms to protect his face. The wolverine caught his shirt, just under his right elbow near his wrist.

The weight of the animal caused Allan to lose his balance, and the two rolled over on the cavern floor together. Allen had one knee jammed against the wolverine's chest, pushing it backwards. He lay partly on his back and tried to wriggle out of the way. The wild beast still had its teeth latched on his shirt, its claws spread across his side; they could eviscerate him in half a second. Allen tried to shove the animal away from him, but the wolverine would not let go.

Ike appeared behind Allen, torch in one hand and pistol in the other. "Look out!" yelled Watson, and then fired a round.

The wolverine released its grip on Allen's sleeve and lunged for his neck. Allen pulled up his revolver. Although it was wild, the shot took the beast directly in the right eye, piercing his brain, and he fell over like a lump of lead, to move no more. For a second, Allen just sprawled on the rocks, catching his breath. His head was spinning.

"A close shave for ye," remarked Watson, "How are ye?"

"I... I guess I am not much hurt!" gasped Allen, when he felt able to speak. "The beast didn't get its teeth into me."

"A big one, too," Ike went on, shoving the wolverine with his boot.

"I find myself in your debt again," Allen said. "Twice you've come along in time to save my life."

"Your shot finished it, not mine. Wolverines can take down a moose. Lucky thing he didn't get yer throat." Ike holstered his weapon and helped Allen to his feet. "I knowed a man once as got a nip there from a wolverine that made him pass in his checks then an' there."

"Well, I thought I was a goner there for sure," Allen breathed out.

"Didn't ye have a torch?"

"I did, but the water put it out." Allen indicated the soggy stick of wood on the ground.

"The darkness was what made the critter so bold," Ike explained. "They're afeared o' fire, just like most o' wild beasts."

"Slavin!" Allen shouted out suddenly. "He's been left by himself! I'll bet you a horse that he's fled."

"Ye're right," exclaimed Ike, "I heard the ruckus back here and just came runnin'."

He began to make his way back to the main cavern at a quick pace, with Allen close beside him. It didn't take but a single glance around to convince them that Slavin had indeed gone.

"Took my other shootin' iron, too, consarn him!" fumed Ike.

"Look!" Allen gestured toward the horses.

"What now?"

"He has taken one of the horses, too!" Allen said.

Allen was right. Slavin and the best of the horses were gone.

Chapter 19

Paul stared at the captured thief. Jeff Jones gloated like a rat who had just stolen the cheese out of the trap.

"So you know something of Captain Grady and our uncle, Barnaby Winthrup?" called out Chet, excitedly. "What is it?"

"That's fer you two fellers to find out...unless you let me go." Jones barely suppressed a smug smile.

Paul knew that the man's bargain was out of the question, but perhaps he could force the information out of him another way. Jones seemed to be the type of person who prided himself on being more intelligent than he actually was. Paul decided that was his point of attack.

"You mean you won't speak unless we free you?" Chet asked the outlaw.

"I figure it that way," Jones flatly declared.

"Don't waste your breath on him, Chet," Paul drawled as he completed patching up the shoulder wound. "He doesn't know nothing."

"That's what you think!" Jones snorted.

"Come on, Chet. Are you going to believe a low-down horse thief?" Paul calmly gathered his supplies and stood. He sauntered to the kitchen to put away the items he borrowed. "Besides, we can't promise anything until Mr. Dottery gets back," he tossed over his shoulder.

"In that case, I ain't talkin'." The prisoner spoke with the cool assurance of somebody who held all the cards.

"If you know anything about our uncle you had better speak out, if you wish us to do anything at all for you," Chet hinted.

"I won't say a word," Jones lowered his voice. "Get rid of the other one. You and I can palaver. Just us two. We can come to an understandin'."

Paul smiled as he observed unseen in the kitchen door. So that was Jones' game: try to play one brother off the other. Well, he'll let him; he'll help him, in fact.

"Oh, let Jack Blowfen take him over to the next camp and tell the men that he's a downright horse thief." Paul came back into the room and stood next to Chet. "Would you fancy that, Jones? You can guess what would happen." He tipped his head to one side while he held one hand over it, uttering a strangling sound.

The gang member's eyes grew wide, but he rapidly recovered. "I ain't afeared."

"Don't you realize what it is to have us able to speak a word for you?" Chet encouraged.

"I told you already, Chet, he's as blind as a snubbin post," Paul dismissed Jones with a wave of his hand. "He's a fool."

"But he said—" Chet began.

Paul watched his younger brother, who appeared to be trying to figure things out. At the same time, he seemed to understand that Paul was on to something. Paul met Chet's gaze and spoke deliberately. "Stop talking to him, Chet, or else I'm going to have to clean your plow."

"What are you doing? Trying to kick a row?"

Paul spat on the floor and pushed up the sleeves of his shirt. "Like you could, mule brains."

After a second, the confusion cleared in Chet's eyes, and he nodded almost imperceptibly. "Yeah? Well, if any plow needs cleaning around here, pardner, yours is the one," Chet snapped.

"You always fall for burro milk," Paul added in disgust.

"Oh, I do, do I? And you're so smart!" Chet spat back.

"I am smarter than you! You always believe nonsense! All the time!" Paul fired back.

"What do you mean by that?" Chet shouted, giving Paul a shove.

"Just what I say!" Paul yelled, pushing Chet back. "You're not only short in stature, but in smarts as well."

Chet screamed in rage and tackled Paul. The two crashed to the floor and rolled around as they grunted and punched at each other, Paul whispering rapid instructions to Chet. Chet wrestled Paul face down and straddled him. He grabbed one of Paul's arms and wrenched it up behind his back.

"No! Not again, Chet! Don't break my arm again! Please! Stop!" Paul pleaded as he pounded the ground with his free fist. He groaned in pain.

"That's what you get for starting it! For such an all-fired smart guy, you never learn nothin'!" Chet released his hold and got to his feet. He kicked Paul in his side. "I'll thank you to stay out of my business! I'll talk to whoever I please, however I please, whenever I want! Understood?"

"Yes, Chet. Of course, Chet. I understand, Chet." Paul whimpered as he rolled over on his back. He noted with satisfaction that Jones had twisted around to watch the bout. Paul scooted into a corner like a wounded animal, cradling his injured arm. "Just don't hurt me again."

Chet stalked to Jones and loomed over him, feet planted and hands held out to his side like claws, panting with exertion.

Jones grinned. "Good for you, boy. That's the way. Now it's just you and me. Now, let me go and I'll tell you all about—"

Chet shook his head. "No. You will tell me first. Right now."

"Nothing doin', youngster. The deal is—"

"I'm growing impatient with you, Jones. Unlike my stupid brother, I think you do have something to say, but I'm getting tired of waiting," Chet growled.

"Don't get him mad, Jones," Paul warned. "He's like a wild beast when he loses his temper. You saw—"

"Shut up, or I'll do more than break your arm again!" Chet barked at Paul. He glared at Jones. "Well, what's your answer? You had better talk, fast and loud. I've been nice to you so far. Haven't I, Paul?"

"Yes, Chet. Very much so. You've been extra special agreeable, Chet." Paul spoke in a timid, weak voice. "I'm warning you, Jones, watch out for him. He can be just plain mean."

"Shall I turn you over to Blowfen?" Chet threatened the thief. "If you don't tell me what I want to know, I'll do that. I'll even slip the noose over your ornery head myself. How would you like that?"

"No! No! Don't let him take me down to the Fork!" howled Jones. "Anything but that!"

"But first, I'm going to make you talk. Remember, I don't need to be kind. Not to him," Chet nodded toward Paul, and jabbed a threatening finger toward the man's bandaged wound, "and certainly not to you. I can undo all that pretty work Paul did on your shoulder. Painfully. Now talk because I'm just itching to go to work." His hands formed into fists.

"I don't know much, but I'll tell you all I do," offered the prisoner, after a short pause, "and you are to do the best you can for me, promise me that?"

"We will," Chet looked over to his brother. "Won't we, Paul?"

"Yes, of course. We give our word." Paul stood.

"Well, Captain Grady has been a-spottin' your uncle fer several weeks—ever since he got Winthrup to leave San Francisco," the prisoner began.

"Got him out San Francisco?" queried Paul. "We reckoned something like that happened."

"Yes. I don't know how the thing was done—" the man started.

Chet cut him off. "We do. Go on."

"Well, somehow he got your uncle to leave the city," Jones continued, "and now he's tryin' to make him give up a secret of a mine, or somethin' like that."

"That explains it all," Chet said to Paul. "Uncle Barnaby must be in Captain Grady's power." He turned his attention back to Jones. "Where's our uncle now?"

The man shook his head. "That I can't say. I tell you the truth."

"Captain Grady must know," Chet prompted.

"Sure he does," Jones confirmed.

Paul came next to Chet. "And by getting us out of our ranch he wanted to make us leave the area." He thought a moment. "I believe Grady might be the head of a band who wish to obtain entire control of this section—land, water, minerals." He turned to Chet. "Oh, yes, I'll wash and dry the dishes next time."

Chet grinned and flexed his biceps. "Brawn over brains! I almost busted up laughing when you pleaded 'don't hurt me again.'"

Jones looked between the two brothers as it dawned on him that they tricked him. He exploded in a flurry of curses.

"Temper, temper." Paul clucked his tongue. "Don't worry. Chet and I will keep our part of the agreement."

"We'll make Grady tell us where he holds uncle, never fear." Chet began to pace. "I wish Mr. Dottery would come back."

"I hear somebody down the road," Paul walked to the door. "They must be coming back now."

Paul was right. A clatter sounded outside and a moment later Caleb Dottery appeared in the doorway, with Jack Blowfen behind.

"Couldn't catch 'em in the dark," Dottery strode into the house and dropped into a simple but comfortable chair, "but thank fortune, the stock is safe!"

"Slippery rascals, Mangle and Nodley," commented Blowfen, "but we'll round 'em up some day, I'll bet my sombrero on it."

"We have just heard valuable news," said Paul, and he repeated what Jones had said.

The rancher and his cowboy helper listened with interest. The former gave a long, soft whistle of astonishment.

"If you are right, Paul," said Dottery, "Grady is a horse thief as great as was old Sol Davids, and he is trying to rob yer uncle out of a mine as well."

"Not only that, but as this fellow said, he is with the crowd who made my uncle a prisoner, sir. That is the worst part of it," put in Chet.

"Must say I didn't quite think it of the captain, though I allow as how he's a slick one," Dottery remarked. "What's to do about it?"

"We came here for your help before all the excitement," said Chet. "Captain Grady already took possession of our ranch tonight. You know he sets up some sort of claim to it."

"Got yer papers, ain't ye?" Dottery leaned forward in his chair.

"No," Paul admitted, "they burned when we had our little fire."

The rancher sat back. "Humph! Bad luck!"

"Nevertheless, the place is ours. Our father bought and paid for it," asserted Paul firmly, "and we intend to move Captain Grady out, even if we have to fight him."

"Good fer ye!" exclaimed Blowfen. "I like the way yer talk. I'm right to lend a hand to ye. I love grit, I do!" He held out his big hand to Paul as if to bind a deal. Paul shook it.

"Ye can count on my help, too," Dottery slapped one knee and stood. "Ye have done a good turn this night which I'm not gonna to forget in a hurry."

"Jeff Jones told us about our uncle and Captain Grady of his own free will," said Paul. "So, if you can be a little easy on him on that account Chet and I wish you would be."

"Stealin' horses ain't no light crime," argued Dottery.

"An' it don't improve a man's reputation to become a sneak," put in Blowfen.

A debate began, with Paul and Chet steadfastly holding up their end of the promise they made with Jones. Dottery and Blowfen finally agreed to hold the thief merely as a prisoner for the present, instead of carrying him to the nearest camp to be turned over to the vigilante committee.

"I'll chain Jones up as a prisoner in the house till we git back," said Dottery, "He'll keep quiet if he knows when he is well off."

"Can we borrow some canvas?" asked Paul.

"Why, sure, there's some in the barn," replied Blowfen.

It was so near morning that to think of retiring was out of the question. Blowfen stirred about getting breakfast, and at six o'clock they dined.

***

Paul, Chet, Dottery and Blowfen were on their horses, riding at a lope away from the house and down the road to the Winthrup ranch. After Jones was locked up, everybody made both house and outbuildings as secure as possible. Paul was in the lead, armed with his rifle and ready for anything. A twist of his neck made his hat brim shade his eyes. The others had guns on their hips and rifles in their scabbards. The horses' hooves kicked up little puffs of dust that drifted up on the wind which fell at the edges of the road.

"I'm curious if Grady is alone or if a number of the gang are with him," wondered Paul as he rode beside his brother, just in front of the two men. He shrugged. "I guess we won't find out until we get there."

"Most likely he's expecting trouble and has help at hand," returned Chet. "He understands well enough we won't give up our ranch without a fight."

"Maybe he thought he'd frighten us off until Allen got back from San Francisco," Paul said.

"Don't make any difference how many men he got," broke in Blowfen. "He ain't no right to put ye out like a couple o' dogs, an' he savvy it."

At a little after noon, the group reached Demon Hollow.

"The Hollow looks different in the daylight, doesn't it?" laughed Paul. "Do you remember your demon, Chet?"

"Yes, indeed." Chet flushed red with embarrassment at the memory.

They passed through the Hollow with no incident. At the creek they stopped to water the animals and eat the lunch which Blowfen had packed up before starting. It was afternoon when they at last came close to the ranch home.

"I see our belongings are still in the road," observed Paul, pointing ahead. He held out his hand to stop the group. "Grady or his men could be waiting for us to show up with help, then open fire." Paul turned toward Dottery and Blowfen. "You two wait here and stay out of sight. Chet and I will approach the house, as if checking on our belongings, and wrap it with the canvas. Grady expects that. At the same time, we'll see if we can spot anybody around the place."

Dottery nodded. "It's your show."

"Come on," Paul motioned to Chet.

"Yes, but Paul—" Chet began.

"Come on, I say," Paul started Jasper toward their house.

Chet followed. When they reached their possessions, they dismounted and made a show of examining everything in the pile.

Paul was irritated that his books and magazines were dumped on the dirt, so he packed them carefully into one of the trunks.

"It looks like rain," Paul nodded towards the black clouds huddled against the mountains. "Must be already storming up there. We got here just in time."

He pulled out the canvas, and with Chet's help, covered their things while throwing searching glances around the area. The ranch appeared deserted. Every building was tightly closed.

"It could be Grady thought better of everything and skipped out," suggested Chet in a low voice.

"Perhaps, but I doubt it," Paul responded in a whisper. "We need to get inside the house, but I don't want to chance trying to walk in the front door. Let's go back to Mr. Dottery."

"At least everything is still here, and it's protected from the rain," Chet said loudly. "Mr. Dottery's wagon should be big enough."

Paul nodded, and the brothers climbed back into their horse's saddles. They rode back to the others.

"Well?" asked Blowfen.

"We think nobody's around," Paul reported, "but we're not sure. We need to get inside."

"Do ye think you can do it?" Dottery glanced toward the ranch house.

"I think so. We can try, anyway," Paul answered.

Dismounting, the brothers made their way to where a deep ditch drained from the ranch home into the river. The trench was almost dry, and all but choked up with weeds and brush.

"The captain may really fire at us, although I think he'll hardly dare do it with Blowfen and Mr. Dottery at hand to see that justice is done," Paul said as they let themselves down into the ditch.

"If he shoots, we'll shoot back," Chet stated grimly. "He has no right on our ranch, and, besides, we must do something for Uncle Barnaby's sake."

Paul and Chet wormed their way along. The ditch led around to the rear of their home, but then went underground. The only cover they had between them and the house was tall grass.

"We must be careful, in case anybody is in the house," Paul whispered.

Chet nodded. They left the ditch and took to the grass, stooping over and running until they were under their bedroom window. Paul cautiously peered inside, then spoke quietly into Chet's ear.

"The room is empty, but the door's ajar," he said. "I can't hear any movement."

Chet grabbed the corner of the window and gave it a quick shake. He pulled it open.

"I'm glad I never fixed this latch like Allen told me to," he said in a soft voice. The two grinned and hoisted themselves over the sill. It was a strange feeling to be standing in their own room, now completely bare. It was almost as though they didn't belong there anymore. The brothers crept to the partially open door, revolvers drawn. Paul opened it slightly to peek into the main room, grimacing at the squeak the hinges let out.

Nobody was there. The captain had moved but a few things into the ranch home—a couple of chairs, a table, and an old trunk. The gun rack still held the family's rifles. Paul concentrated, but the only other thing he heard was the blood pounding in his ears. He motioned Chet toward the kitchen, then walked toward Allen's room and looked in. It only held a bed.

Chet stepped back into the room and shook his head while he jerked his thumb back toward the kitchen. Paul slid along the wall to the storage room. He paused a second, then threw open the door. Empty.

"Grady must have flown the coop," Chet said as he holstered his gun and walked up to Paul, "but he must have had several visitors recently. A number of unwashed dishes and drinking glasses are stacked by the stove. Plus some empty bottles."

Paul slipped his gun back in its holster and knelt in front of the trunk. "I wonder why he brought this along."

"Clothes, I expect," Chet shrugged.

Paul opened the trunk, revealing bundles of documents. "Can't wear these." He pulled out the top paper and scanned it. "Interesting ..."

"Well, what is it?" Chet peeked over Paul's shoulder.

"A deed that releases all our claims to the ranch, complete with places for us to sign," Paul explained. "I guess Grady wants to make his swindle as legal-looking as he can." Paul worked his way down the stack of documents as carefully as possible.

"Why are you being so neat?" Chet complained. "Hurry up, dump all that stuff on the floor, so we can check it out."

Paul shook his head. "These must be important. Grady wouldn't decamp and leave all them here, so he must be returning. I don't want him to grow suspicious because he discovers that the contents have been disturbed."

"If those are so all-fire vital, why didn't he lock the trunk?" Chet asked.

Paul shrugged. "Arrogance of power, I suspect. He thinks quite highly of himself. Or perhaps he's planning to use our ranch as the headquarters of his operation. Maybe he simply didn't believe we would return." He extracted another folded document from lower in the stack and opened it. "It's a plan of this section. Look, there is an X marked on our ranch, and on Mr. Dottery's. There are dates written on them, too." He examined the paper closely. "The date on Mr. Dottery's ranch is yesterday! And there are notes on other properties."

"Do you think it means anything?"

"I thought it odd that we got hit by the horse thieves, and a short time later, so did Mr. Dottery. This map proves those raids were not a coincidence. The attempt on Mr. Dottery was the same day as marked here, as well as ours." Paul checked the paper he held again and tapped it. He thought a moment. "Maybe this is 'Captain' Grady's battle plan. He's targeting Mr. Dottery and our spreads first, since we both border his. Try this: perhaps Grady's first step in taking over a piece of land is to use the leftovers from the Sol Davids gang to steal all the ranch's livestock, as well as any money they can find. Not having enough cash to replace the animals, the rancher goes broke. Grady then swoops in to acquire the property on the cheap." Paul gave the map to Chet and dug a little deeper into the trunk. He delicately extracted another paper like a dentist pulling a tooth and read it. "Well, well, well."

"What have you got there?" Chet refolded the map.

"A bill of sale for this land from Sam Slater," Paul said.

"What!" Chet cried in shock, "Grady is right? He does own our ranch?"

"Here's where Slater signed," Paul pointed to a flowing signature at the bottom of the page. "Except there is one problem."

"A problem? What?"

"Sam Slater couldn't write."

Chet gasped. "He couldn't?"

"Neither read or write. He marked our bill of sale—the real one—with an X. I remember seeing it." Paul handed the paper to Chet. "This is a forgery. I think we will be correct in making Captain Grady a prisoner."

"Why didn't Grady just put our names to that other claim? Fake them, like he did Slater?"

"We've signed other things," Paul said after reflecting for a moment, "like cattle sales contracts, credit slips at the store, receipts, and so on. All of us attended school for a bit. It would be an easy matter to find other samples of our signatures and writing to compare them. Chet, take those documents to Mr. Dottery, and explain what we've found. Ask him and Blowfen to carry them and Jones to the sheriff, then bring the lawman back to his place. We'll wait for them there. Go out the way we came in. Quickly."

"The captain is nailed to the counter!" Chet grinned as he stuck the papers in his pocket and dashed from the room.

Paul returned to the trunk, where he found even more letters. The documents clearly revealed the captain's true character and schemes. Paul smiled to himself to think how foolish the rascal had been not to have destroyed the papers.

"He must be saving them for when he writes his memoirs," Paul said to himself sarcastically. "But the greatest of villains occasionally over-reach themselves. There is proof enough here to show what an awfully bad man Captain Grady is." Paul made sure nothing seemed to have been touched in the trunk, then closed the lid by the time Chet returned.

"Mr. Dottery and Blowfen left," Chet told Paul. "They'll do what you asked."

"Good. Let's get out of here." The two went through their room and climbed out the window, closing it again.

"What do we have here?"

A voice sounded from behind them. The brothers spun around. Mangle and Nodley faced them, guns pointed.

"A couple of sneak thieves, I wager," sneered Nodley.

"Where did you two come from?" demanded Chet.

"Why, we're the men from the moon!" Mangle chortled as Nodley joined in.

"We sees the four of you comin', so we hides in the cottonwoods there," Nodley said nodding toward the stand of trees a little behind the house, "and waited until your pals left."

Mangle peered at Chet. "Wait a minute! Yer the youngster we schooled when you followed us! Ain't he, Darry?"

Nodley hooted. "He sure enough is!"

"Now we just waits until the captain gets back." Mangle smiled. "I'm sure he'll want to do some jawin' with you youngsters. Then maybe it'll be time for more schoolin'."

Chapter 15

Allen and Ike stood at the entrance of the cave, peering into the storm.

"He ain't got much o' a start," observed Ike. "So let's get after him hot-footed."

"I'm with you on that, Ike," agreed Allen. "He must not escape under any circumstances. If he does—"

"We won't be able to get on the trail o' yer uncle," Ike finished.

Allen swallowed the lump in this throat. He nodded, then pulled himself up to his full height. Tightening his collar with one hand to attempt to keep out the rain, he strode to his horse.

Both Allen and Ike were soon in the saddle and away. They dashed into the storm, the dreary late afternoon grayness punctuated by flashes of lightning and rumble of thunder. Tracking under such a situation wasn't easy, but they managed to spot some tracks in the soft dirt in front of the cliff. These led to a back trail where the ravine widened between the rocky slopes of the mountains. The storm continued, bringing a heavy rain that poured down steadily, but Allen refused to give up.

"He must not escape," Allen repeated to himself, over and over again, almost as a command. "We must capture him and make him take us to where the gang holds Uncle Barnaby a prisoner."

"Right ye are, Allen," Ike threw over his shoulder.

Allen gave a start. He didn't realize he had said anything out loud.

After covering a half a mile, Ike called a halt. "Ye want to go easy here," he cautioned, "I don't like the looks o' this territory nohow."

"What's wrong?" Allen tried to pierce the slashing rain.

"Full o' holes, for one thing, and water under the surface. We'll go slow," Ike warned.

They moved forward cautiously, allowing their horses to pick their way along the difficult path. Trees to their right and left made out a fringe, and every so often the lightning illuminated their waving branches. The wind swept through them, creating a sad, dirge-like sound.

Allen and Ike continued haltingly when they heard a sudden yell ahead: Slavin calling to his horse.

"Back up!" came another shout. "Back, hang ye! De ye want ter pitch me in a hole?" A savage muttering they could not make out followed.

"We've got him!" exclaimed Ike. "Come—but be careful, be careful."

"I'm going to dismount. It may be safer." Allen did so and led Lily along the trail made slippery and treacherous by the puddling water.

Ike likewise got down, and they scanned the area in front of them. Allen shivered as the rain ran down his neck and back.

"There!" Allen pointed ahead.

"Where? What's happened?" asked the old hunter.

"Both Slavin and the horse have gone down."

"Now we've got the rascal sure!"

The trail narrowed, with a deep gully on one side, and a fringe of thick brush on the other. A faint groan echoed off the mountains.

"The fall hurt him." Allen handed Lily's reins to Ike. "Look after my horse, will you? I am going to scout ahead."

He hurried as fast as he dared around a tight turn of the trail, avoiding the branches and leaves of bushes clustered close to the lip of the hollow. As he emerged from the growth, he saw the dangerous situation before him.

Slavin had fallen over the edge of the trail at a point where a huge half-rotted tree lay. It had slipped in the wet, rolled partly over the man, and slowly but surely was crushing the life out of him.

"Slavin!" Allen cried.

"Hel—help!" begged the injured man. "Help! For the love of Heaven, help me!"

"How did you end up under the trunk?" Allen moved closer to the edge of the trail.

"My horse kicked me and I fell. I tried to stop myself from going into the hollow. Please help me!" Slavin's sentence ended in a groan.

Ike appeared next to Allen. "See what ye get for runnin' away."

"Ike, not now," Allen snapped.

"Don't talk! Save me!" pleaded Slavin.

"We'll do what we can for you," assured Allen.

As he spoke, he realized how difficult, not to mention dangerous, was the task which lay before them. He sized up the situation, trying to work out a plan. As Allen saw it, he needed a way to remove the injured Slavin from under the log. If Allen attempted to roll or move the trunk, it might catch him as surely as Slavin.

The tree originally grew on the gully side of the trail. When it toppled over, a tangle of roots, like skeletal fingers clutching out of a grave, stuck up at the edge.

"Ike, can you grab on one of those roots? Try to keep the tree from going any farther into the ravine?" Allen asked as he pointed. He removed his gun belt and hung it over Lily's saddle horn.

"I can try. Wait till I tether the horses."

This was done as rapidly as possible and the old hunter caught hold of one of the roots. Making sure of his footing, Allen started inching down the slope sideways.

"Take care!" advised Ike. "The bank here is mighty slippery."

"Tell me something I don't know!" Allen fired back.

Allen planted his feet and slowly worked his way down the embankment. A lightning bolt struck a nearby tree's tallest branches and splintered it into several large pieces. The rain pounded down heavier than ever, almost drowning out the boom of the thunderclap and filling the air with the sweet, wet scent of water. Startled, Allen lost his footing, and the mud gave way. He started to slide downhill. He dropped flat on his stomach to stop his downward momentum, his fingers and boots sinking into the mud until he came to a halt. For a moment everything went silent. Allen took a deep breath and coughed up mud.

"Allen?" Ike hollered.

"I'm all right!" Allen got on his hands and knees and crawled backward to where Slavin lay trapped. When he reached the trunk, he clung to it as he moved to the down slope side. He caught the injured man by the arm.

"Can't you turn over?" Allen asked Slavin.

"I... I...can't budge!" was the low answer, and then with a moan the prisoner passed out.

"He's fainted!" called Allen to Ike. "Pull on that root for all you are worth! Can you move it?"

"I'm a-pullin'," came a strained reply.

The tree did not shift, with one end stuck in the mud lying on the edge of the bank.

Allen planted his feet in the muck, flexed his knees, and put his back against the log. Taking a deep breath, he pushed. The trunk moved in a bit but shoved him in return. He stumbled face-first into a puddle of brown water and thought he was going to drown for a second.

"Hold fast, Ike!" Allen instructed as he spat out some water. "I'm going to try something else!"

"Ye can't do nothin', Allen," protested the old hunter. "Come away afore the tree rolls over an' crushes ye too!"

"It won't roll if you hold fast!" Allen urged.

"Yes, it will, if it starts," Ike argued. "I got nothin' to brace ag'in here!"

"Well, I'm going to do my best and you must hang on as long as you can!" Allen ordered.

Getting down on his knees, Allen began to scoop away the loose ground with his hands, working directly under Slavin's body. He clawed at the wet earth, his fingers ripping clods of muck as he dug. The work was hard as he dug deeper into the ground and discovered wetter, sloppy layers of soil. The mud was slippery and oozed into the area he just cleared, but he kept on. At last the hole underneath Slavin grew deep enough to reach the trapped man.

"Now hold tight, I'm going to pull Slavin out!" he yelled to Ike.

"I'm tryin'!" bellowed the old hunter

Allen pulled with all his strength, and at last the senseless body of Slavin came free from the trap.

"Quick, the tree is a-goin'!" came a loud warning from Ike. "I can't hold on any longer!"

Grunting, his heart pounding with exertion, Allen started dragging Slavin's dead weight around the end of the trunk.

"Allen! Watch out!" shouted Ike. "It got away from me!"

The tree began to shake, then slip down the bank. With a yell, Allen straightened his legs and pulled up with all his might. He fell backwards into the mud, Slavin's body on top of him. The trunk picked up speed, grazed past them, and tumbled into the gully. The mud clung to his back, slippery as ice and heavy like a rock.

"Allen!"

"Here, Ike! We're all right!"

Allen shifted Slavin to his right, then brought up his knees. Setting his boots in the mire, he wriggled himself up the slope like a snake, pulling the unconscious body along with him. He repeated this maneuver a couple of times until he ended up slightly below the rim of the trail.

"Give me yer hand!" Ike knelt on the ground above Allen.

Allen reached and grasped Ike's hand. As Ike pulled, Allen continue to work his way up, until he and Slavin sprawled safe on level earth once more.

"A close call an' no error!" Ike commented, "Ye came within an ace o' goin' into the hollow with the tree on top o' ye!"

"I think Slavin's pretty badly hurt," said Allen, when he could catch his breath. "That trunk had him pinned down for fair. He would have been crushed in another minute or two. What should we do with him?"

"Wait till I get his mount an' we'll take him back to the cave," suggested Ike.

To catch the animal was not difficult and close at hand they found the gun Slavin took. While Allen carried the firearms and led one horse and rode another, Watson took up the senseless man in his arms and followed on his own mount to the cavern.

They placed the injured man in a comfortable position near the fire, which Ike heaped up with fresh wood, so that all might dry themselves. Allen brought the horses inside and tethered them to what remained of the branch. He plucked another burning brand from the fire and headed to the rear of the cave where he encountered the wolverine.

As he stepped into the area with the waterfall and underground lake, he hesitated, throwing a nervous glance toward the body of the animal. In the flickering shadows thrown by his torch, he thought he saw it stir, a red, evil light gleaming in its eye. He shook his head. No, it was dead, and would stay dead. He commanded himself not to look at the beast.

He stripped off his clothes and used the falling water to shower off as much of the mud as he could, then rinsed out his clothes in the lake as best he was able. He slipped on his pants, then with one last look back at the wolverine, grabbed his shirt and boots, and returned to the fire. Placing them close to the flames, he huddled near it himself.

At least a half hour more passed before Slavin opened his eyes to stare about him.

"I... I...where am I?" he stammered.

"Yer outta danger," remarked Watson, laconically.

Slavin licked his lips. "That tree... Did I go over into the hollow?"

"No," Ike said.

"How did I escape?"

Ike nodded toward Allen. He sat by the fire, holding his shirt toward the flames to dry it. "Allen Winthrup there saved ye."

"He did!"

"Yes, Slavin; he's yer best friend, if ye only know it," went on the old hunter.

"But I...don't...don't understand."

In a few words Ike told of the rescue to Slavin. The injured man rested his eyes on Allen.

"I'm much obliged to ye," he said deliberately. His manner showed he meant it.

Slavin's words made Allen feel uncomfortable, almost embarrassed. He curtly nodded an acknowledgment to the expression of gratitude.

"You were a fool to try to skedaddle," continued Ike.

"I know that...now," muttered the injured man.

"Don't ye know I would have plugged ye on sight?" Ike demanded.

"Would ye have?"

"Certain sure, Slavin," Ike said bluntly.

"Well, I won't give ye another chance," Slavin said with a heavy sigh.

"There won't be another, ye mean," threatened the old hunter.

"All right, just as ye please, Watson. But if that young feller saved my life, why I'm..." Slavin's voice faltered.

"What?" Ike prompted.

Slavin looked at Allen. "I'm going to make it up to you. I promise."

"I take that to understand that you will lead us to my uncle without any further trouble?" questioned Allen. He squeezed his shirt a few times to check if it was completely dry, then slipped it on.

Slavin nodded. "I will do that, an' I'll swear to it if ye want me to."

"You don't need to, Slavin." Allen pulled on his boots.

"But I mean it, Winthrup. I may be a bad man, but I ain't so all-fired bad as to forget a man when he does me a good turn," the outlaw said.

Allen stood and buttoned his shirt. "Fine, I will take you at your word."

"But I can't go on right yet. I got a terrible pain in my breast, here." Slavin tapped his chest.

"I don't doubt you have," Allen noted dryly. "We won't move tonight and maybe not tomorrow. It will depend upon how you feel. Anyway, I think a little rest here will be a benefit to us all."

"Yes, ye all need it," acknowledged Ike. "An' now I want all o' ye to turn in an' grab some sleep. I'll stay on guard."

"But not all night," insisted Allen. "Wake me at two or three o'clock."

Allen went on duty at three o'clock and leaned against one side of the cave opening. The rain still came down in cold sheets, and Allen couldn't help but worry about his two younger brothers. How were Chet and Paul doing? With all they have to be on guard about out there night and day, would they know who to trust? Could they handle running the ranch by themselves without him?

Could they deal with Grady if he returned? He wished he could be them.

Allen thought about his uncle and what might happen when they found him. He had probably suffered a great deal, and he might be suffering at this very moment. What condition would he be in? Would he be injured? Would taking care of him be added to Allen's chores of looking after Paul, Chet and the ranch?

The thought of more responsibilities falling on him was too heavy for his shoulders to bear and felt like the weight of the mountain itself pressed down. After a moment, a saying of Paul's popped into Allen's mind.

"We'll cross that bridge when we get to it," Allen whispered aloud. He took a deep breath, straightened up and spoke aloud again. "I'll cross that bridge when I get to it."

Turning his back on the rain, he went inside the cavern and remained on guard until six, when the others awoke.

An hour later, the sun showed itself in the east and a few scattering drops was all that was left over from the storm. By the time Ike arose, Allen had breakfast ready and all ate without delay. Even Slavin got around, but it was plain that he was suffering.

"I want to show ye I mean to do what I said," he told Allen. His voice was weak. "I'll go on until I drop in my tracks."

"We won't start just yet, Slavin," Allen said gently, "and when we do, we'll take it rather easy, for your benefit."

It was past eight o'clock when the group left the cave. Their horses refreshed by the rest taken, they made good progress along the foothills despite Slavin's injuries.

The section of the state through which they traveled was lonely and Allen could not help mentioning this fact to Ike. The old hunter merely laughed at his words.

"Lonely," he snorted. "Gosh all hemlock, Allen, it ain't half as lonely as it used to be, not by a jugful. Why, I remember the time ye could ride for days an' days an' see nothin' but buffalo or some other wild critters."

Talking over one thing and another the party moved along until about eleven o'clock, when they decided to find a place where they could halt to eat. Allen noticed that Slavin, however, was pale.

"You need a rest, Slavin," he said kindly.

"I reckon ye air right," came the faint response. He tried to smile. "Didn't calculate for such an all-gone feelin'."

"We'll take it easy until the worst of the heat is over; eh, Ike?" Allen called over his shoulder.

"Jes' as ye say," answered Ike.

They found an inviting place in a small grove of pine trees. The spot by a spring and brook was shaded, so Allen assisted Slavin to the ground and then joined Ike, who had already settled himself under another tree a little way off.

"He's a changed man, unless I miss my guess," said Allen to Ike in a quiet voice.

"I think ye are right, Allen," Ike nodded, "That adventure took him so near the big jump I reckon it tickled his conscience."

"I hope he does turn over a new leaf. He doesn't appear such a bad fellow at heart." Allen lay back against the tree trunk and tilted his hat over his eyes. "I suppose some men go bad out here simply because are no good examples to follow. They cut loose from their old associates and fall in with the wrong people."

"That's just it, and it's easier to find the bad sort than the right sort," Ike said. "Some men think life altogether too slow 'less they are doin' somethin' against the law."

"Like Captain Grady." Allen pushed his hat back. He sat forward, his eyes blazing with fury. "Like what his henchmen are doing to Uncle Barnaby."

"It may not be as bad as ye imagine, Allen," said Ike. "Yer uncle knows a thing or two."

"Of course he does," Allen picked up a stick and angrily snapped it in two, "but one man can't do much against three or four, or half a dozen. Those villains will do all in their power to bring him to terms, you can be certain of that."

Allen flung the sticks away. The two were silent for several minutes.

"Well, I'm ready to push on at any time ye say," said Ike.

"We'll move on as fast as Slavin can travel. We can't do more than that," Allen responded. "If he cashes in on our hands, we'll have no means of finding out anything more about my uncle's whereabouts."

"He ain't shamming, is he?" Ike wondered.

Allen shook his head. "Not a bit of it. He was caught under the tree and I wouldn't have been in his position for a thousand dollars."

"Then we won't push him any harder than you dare." Ike glanced over to Slavin, tossing and turning in his sleep, beads of sweat appearing on his forehead. "To me he looks like a fellow who might be gettin' a fever."

"I saw that. But I hope he doesn't," concluded Allen.

His hopes were dashed when they returned to Slavin. He was in a bad way.

"Let me go! Take the tree from me!" He sat up and began to talk wildly, eyes open but unfocused. "I haven't got the money! Oh, how do ye do Mr. Winthrup? Glad to see me, eh? And how is that new mine, an' what kind of trade are ye goin' to make with Captain Grady, eh? Ha! Ha! The cave by the seven pines! A good hiding place, the seven pines! Let me go, the tree is crushing me!" And then he fell back almost exhausted.

"Did you hear what he said about the seven pines?" asked Allen. "The cave must be at a place called the seven pines, or near seven trees. Have you heard of such a place?"

"Can't fool me on a thing like this," Ike said, flatly. "Once I see a place it hangs in my mind forever. Same way with trails. Why once I struck one in the south o' the state, kind o' a mixed trail too. I didn't see that area for nigh to six years, but when I did see it ag'in I knew it just as quick as I clapped eyes on it."

"I believe you," replied the young ranchman. "You have eyes like a hawk."

"If they are, I think I know the spot." Ike rubbed his beard as he thought. "I ran across 'em seven pines three ... no, four years ago." He took in the area with a searching look, then nodded. "They are about two, maybe three miles from here, but on the other side o' the mountain. We'll have to go around to get to 'em. But we won't travel any more, not just yet. He's up ag'in a long spell o' sickness."

"Slavin won't go farther at all," Allen declared.

Ike looked at Allen and cocked an eyebrow. "He won't?"

Allen shook his head. "Ike, take Slavin back to Daddy's hotel. Make sure that he gets a doctor."

"I don't know that he'll make it."

"Neither do I, but please try," Allen said. "If he doesn't … if he doesn't, take care of things, will you?"

"Sure I will. I understand. What about ye?"

"I'm heading for that cave," Allen said.

"But, Allen—"

"Ike, I'm so close, the closest I've been in months," Allen said fervently. "I can't turn back now. I have to complete my journey. I have to."

"I savvy," Ike smiled and clapped Allen on his back. "Yer pa would be proud."

"I hope so," Allen smiled. "Thank you for helping Slavin. I can never repay you for all you've done."

The young rancher climbed into his saddle and headed Lily toward the direction he hoped his search would end.

Chapter 16

Chet and Paul lay hogtied on the rough, splintered floor of their ranch's tool shed. After Nodley and Mangle tied them up and deposited them here, the brothers squirmed to move back-to-back. They pushed hard against the other, trying to find a loose end in the knots. They both tried to undo each other's wrists and ankles, but it was impossible because of the way they were tied. The two finally gave up, discouraged, as rain started to drum on the tin roof.

It must have been hours later that Grady, Mangle and Nodley's voices floated in conversation through an open window from inside the house, mixed in with coarse laughter. Still, no one went to check on Chet and Paul. The captain evidently did not want to get wet in order to visit his captive guests.

Despite the situation the brothers found themselves in, the lack of sleep from the previous night caught up with them. They both drifted off.

Some noise woke Chet later. He had no idea what time it was, but he could tell the light of day was visible through the cracks in the wall boards. He flexed his fingers. They tingled; the ropes around his wrists restricted circulation to his hands. His muscles ached from being unable to move. Shifting around, he saw that Paul was also awake.

The scraping repeated, sounding like removing a barricade. Chet and Paul blinked in the bright sunlight streaming in when the door was flung open. Mangle and Nodley stepped in.

"I hopes you liked yer accommodations," Mangle bowed in mock politeness.

Nodley snickered. "Me, too."

"The captain may wants to see you two." Mangle said.

Mangle cut the rope attaching each brother's bound hands and feet together. Chet and Paul were lifted into the air by the two men and carried outside. The ground was muddy from the rain. They stood the boys in a puddle by front of the porch.

"You two stay right there and don't move," Mangle told Chet and Paul, barely holding back his laughter at his jest. "I'm goin' find out when the captain wants to palaver with you. Keep an eye on 'em, Nodley." He waggled a finger in a mock scolding. "Now don't let 'em run off."

Nodley giggled as leaned against one of the posts. "I won't."

Mangle clumped inside the house.

The brothers stood, baking in the sun which scorched from the blue sky, drying Chet like leather. His thighs hurt from trying to maintain balance with his feet bound together. Beads of sweat broke out on his forehead and under his arms, tickling as they dripped down. A fly landed on his shoulder and crawled across his neck.

About an hour later, the front door opened and Grady sauntered on to the porch, like a king granting an audience. Mangle came behind him, holding a mug of steaming coffee. He handed it to the captain. Grady took a sip and stared at the boys.

"What does this mean?" he demanded sullenly after a pause.

"That we have come to take possession of our own," shouted Chet. "We told you that we would be back."

Captain Grady's laugh was harsh and condescending. "You monkey! *I* have possession o' *you*—two sneakin', no account trespassers! It's ag'inst the law, and I'll have the sheriff on you!"

"You are the trespasser," Paul returned in his placid way. "You have no right to this property."

"I got possession o' this ranch, which rightfully belongs to me, and I mean to keep it," came Grady's forceful reply.

"We deny your rights," Paul responded.

"That makes no difference! I know what's what," Grady flung back.

"Your claim is false," Paul said. "It's fabricated."

"Oh, my! Did you catch that? Listen to the high-falutin' young savage!" Grady spread his hands wide. He held up two fingers at the back of his head as if he wore a feathered headdress. "He talk-um with heap big words he learnt in wigwam! 'Fab-ree-caa-ted!'"

Mangle and Nodley chortled, while Captain Grady basked in their glowing response to his joke.

Paul waited until they finished. "The word means made up."

"I know what it means," Grady hissed back savagely.

"Good. I just wanted to make sure we understood each other," Paul said. "I didn't want to confuse you with words longer than one syllable."

Grady scowled and dashed the contents of his mug at Paul. Paul winced and bent over as the coffee scalded him. He lost his bAllence and toppled into the mud, much to Mangle and Nodley's amusement.

The captain moved to the edge of the porch and indicated Paul. He addressed the other men. "This young savage ain't treatin' his betters like he should. He's a-needin' some teachin' on proper respect."

"My ma washed my mouth out with soap, if I said somethin' disrespectful," Mangle offered.

Grady smiled and nodded.

Mangle walked over to Paul. "Right. Leave it to me."

He dragged Paul to the full rain barrel which stood at the corner of the porch. He got hold of Paul's hair and dunked his head into the green algae-covered water. Bubbles exploded when Paul couldn't hold his breath any longer. Mangle pulled Paul's head up, his hair dripping. Rivulets of water ran down Paul's face and neck.

"Let's see if he a-learned anything," smirked Grady. "Young savage, what is my rank? I'll a-help you. Call me 'captain.'"

"No," Paul replied, his chest heaving as he gasped for air.

Grady turned red in the face and sputtered out something inarticulate. He made an angry gesture to Mangle.

"Still a savage. Needs more learnin'," Mangle announced. He pushed Paul's head back in the water and held him under a bit longer before yanking him back upright.

"Call me 'captain,' young savage," Grady ordered, his voice dark and malevolent.

"No."

Paul managed only a couple of gulps of oxygen before being immersed again. Water splashed over the edge of the barrel as he fought Mangle's grip. Grady moved over for a closer look. Mangle lifted Paul's head slightly above the water level.

"Call me 'captain'!" Grady raged.

"Never."

Mangle doused Paul again and pulled him erect. Paul stared at the captain with overwhelming hatred. Chet had never seen that expression on Paul before, and he gasped. Even Grady instinctively took a step back. Paul spat a mouthful of water at Grady.

The captain vibrated in rage. He threw the mug, striking Paul in the head. "Drown the rat!" he bellowed.

Mangle shoved Paul's head back in the water and pushed down.

"Stop it! Leave him alone!" Chet screamed.

Paul squirmed in Mangle's grip.

"If you kill him," Chet went on urgently, "we can't help you get the ranch. We'll give you the land. We'll do whatever you want."

Paul's struggling grew less violent.

"We'll get out the area, peaceable. We'll talk to Allen. We'll make him agree," Chet pleaded.

Paul's thrashings weakened almost to the point of ceasing.

Chet's desperation led to a strength he never knew he possessed. His voice turned firm and intense. "But if you murder Paul, Allen will never go along with you. He will take revenge on you. He won't give up. You don't know Allen. If it takes him the rest of his life, he'll find you and put you in your grave."

Grady's head snapped toward Chet as if considering the deal. He gestured to Mangle. Mangle released Paul, and his limp form slumped to the ground.

Chet watched his brother for any sign of movement, anything at all, trying to will life back into him. For what seemed to be an eternity, nothing happened. Suddenly, Paul's body convulsed, and he took a deep breath then several more, coughing and vomiting water, retching until he appeared to be breathing normally again.

"I may be a-usin' the monkey and the young savage by and by," Grady told Mangle and Nodley.

"Well, what do we do with 'em?" Nodley asked.

Grady waved his hand in a sign of disinterest as he turned to go inside. "Just don't kill 'em."

There was a dangerous quiet while Mangle and Nodley stared at the brothers. Mangle nudged Nodley.

"Why lookee here," Mangle commented as he pointed to the muddy Paul. "A piggy got outta his sty."

Nodley walked up to Chet and pushed him into the mud.

"Two piggies," Nodley chortled, and he oinked a few times.

Mangle snorted back, picking up Paul's feet. "Dirty piggies!"

Nodley grabbed Chet's feet. "Yeah, bad little piggies."

They dragged the brothers through the muck while making pig noises, snorting and jeering. They flipped the brothers face down and pulled them around some more before turning them back over. Mangle and Nodley released the boys' feet, made their way back to the porch and sat on the steps. They laughed raucously and slapped each other on their backs, finally stopping to catch their breath. The two grinned and pointed at Chet and Paul.

Mangle glanced down at his feet. "Aw, dang. My boots are all covered with mud!"

"Mine too!" Nodley pouted.

"I can't tromp that stuff all over the captain's nice floors!" Mangle complained, jerking his thumb toward the front door. "The boss wouldn't like that!"

Nodley shook his head. "Nope, he surely won't."

"What we needs is some rags to clean 'em with," Mangle rubbed his chin in an exaggerated show of thinking.

"Hmmm. Now where can we get some?" Nodley asked, imitating Mangle's gestures.

The two exchanged glances, smiled, then looked to the boys.

"Why, I know where I can get my hands on 'em!" Mangle stood, followed by Nodley.

The outlaws jerked Chet and Paul to their feet. Mangle whipped out his knife and cut the shirt off Paul's back. Chet's shirt was ripped off as well. The men plopped down on the steps with the garments.

Mangle began wiping his boots. "This rag sure works just dandy!"

"Likewise mine!" Nodley agreed as he worked on his footwear. "I'd say it's the best I ever used!"

They continued, sometimes snapping the soggy shirts to splatter mud on Chet and Paul.

"Why, look!" Mangle exclaimed happily as he buffed his boots. "There so clean, I can see my face!"

"And it is for sure ugly!" Nodley hooted.

The two guffawed. They wadded up the shirts and threw them at the boys. Mangle whispered to Nodley, who grinned and went in the house. Mangle pulled Chet over to the tool shed and stood him against one wall, then positioned Paul next to him.

"All you alright?" Chet asked Paul.

"Yes," Paul uttered. He coughed a couple of times. "We have to hold on until Mr. Dottery gets back with the sheriff."

Nodley popped out of the house, waving two empty bottles. At Mangle's nod of approval, he balanced them on the boys' heads.

"Now don't move a muscle," the outlaw lectured in false sternness.

The two men took a position about ten feet in front of Chet and Paul and drew their weapons.

"Don't let them win," Paul spoke out of the corner of his mouth. "Don't react."

Chet cast a sidelong glance at Paul. His older brother assumed the expressionless appearance of a plaster statue.

"I don't know if I can," Chet said in a quiet voice.

"You can," Paul assured him.

Chet swallowed hard, working at taming his jittery insides.

Mangle swaggered back and forth, making a great performance of finding the right spot to take aim. "Watch this."

"Ah, you can't even hit the wall!" Nodley goaded.

"No?" Mangle squeezed off a shot. It shattered the board next to Chet's left ear.

Chet's bowels felt as if a herd of buffalo was stampeding around down there, but he forced himself not to flinch. He almost smiled at his success. He could do this.

"You call that shootin'?" jeered Nodley as he waved his gun.

Mangle slapped Nodley on the arm. "Ah, the sun was in my eyes! Let's see ye do better."

Nodley playfully blew on the end of his pistol, grinned and pointed the weapon. He fired. A hole opened up in the wall next to Paul's left eye, the flying splinters slicing his cheek.

Paul didn't respond.

Chet thought Mangle appeared irritated at their lack of reaction. He and Paul were winning.

"Ye can't hold a candle to me! Watch this!" Mangle glared at the brothers and fired again.

The bullet struck the wall between Chet and Paul. Their faces did not change.

Mangle roared in anger, emptied his gun at the two, sending fragments of wood skittering and flying through the air like a swarm of insects. Mangle holstered his gun, then grabbed Nodley's revolver and fired off its remaining rounds.

When the blue smoke drifted away, Chet and Paul hadn't moved. Their expressions were unchanged. The bottles remained on their heads. Mangle stalked up to his living targets, as furious as if he had discovered them cheating at cards.

"You missed," Paul said evenly.

"Not even close," Chet added calmly.

Mangle growled and smashed the glass bottles against each other. Chet and Paul closed their eyes to shield them from the flying shards. When they looked back, Mangle was clutching the broken necks of the bottles. He jammed one jagged glass edge into Chet's stomach, then another into Paul's. He smiled at the brothers, his teeth crooked and stained, and twisted the glass. The brothers cried out in pain.

"There now, youngsters, that's better," Mangle said in an ominous growl, "Get ready, a hog-killin' time is just startin'."

Chapter 17

The ride around the mountain was a trying one, forcing Allen to slow down from a gallop to a walk. In some spots the trail was cut up and mired with deep mud, while in others he had to pick his way over stones which were as smooth as they were dangerous.

He paused on a spur of rocks at the lip of a canyon at least five hundred feet deep. Allen drew back after looking into the yawning depth.

"Look at that," Allen said to himself. "Here's a fall for you! If a fellow should tumble here, he would never live to tell it. This would be a bad trail to follow in the dark."

Allen recalled Paul's experience with the Black Rock River gorge. When he started thinking about how he had reacted, the shame and guilt rushed back over him. He resolved he would apologize to Paul as soon as he returned home.

Cautiously stepping back from the edge of the cliff, Allen mounted his horse and turned to the northwest, plunging through a forest of cedar and hemlock. The numerous wild birds here tempted him to bring some of them down with his gun, but he decided against it.

No use making too much noise, he thought. *Remember, somebody may be on guard up at that cave.*

He drew closer to where the old hunter told him he had seen seven pine trees years ago. To Allen, not used to a life in the open country, remembering such a locality would have been difficult, if not impossible, but Ike Watson didn't have that problem.

The sun had sunk lower when Allen rode out at the edge of a valley and stopped to look at the hills across the canyon. He shielded his eyes with one hand and examined the area. He spotted something, taking a sharp intake of breath.

"Is that them?" he mumbled to himself. He gave a long look then sat upright in his saddle. He spoke out loud. "It looks like them—seven pines, sure enough! But where on earth is the cave?"

He decided that it must be nearby, and he wanted to find it before nightfall. He headed Lily downhill, and soon they were making their way through the brush beside the foothills at the base of the mountain. Allen stopped short when he caught sight of something: some broken bushes and marks on the ground.

"If that isn't a pretty fresh trail unless I miss my guess," he muttered. "Probably not over twenty-four hours old, nohow. I reckon I have got it about right." Allen stood in his stirrups. "But I still see nothing of a cave."

He thought about it for a second. The cavern may not be exactly next to the pines, but in sight of them. It seemed likely that the newer trail led to his destination. He followed the tracks to the left.

He struck out with increased confidence. As he progressed, he checked the hoof marks from time to time and grew positive two horsemen had passed that way not long ago. Just as he reached the end of the foothills, he found himself at a mountain water course, and the abrupt finish to the trail. Allen crossed to the other side of the stream. There were no prints visible on the ground.

"I'm stumped now," he sighed.

He listened to the old hunter speaking in his mind: "I ain't a-givin' up jes' yet."

"No, neither am I," Allen replied out loud, "but where did they go?"

Ike's trick from trailing Bluckburn and Slavin came to Allen's memory. He slid off his horse, put his feet into the water, and bent over to look for any evidence of horseshoe prints. The current didn't move swiftly, and it didn't take long for him to pick up the imprints in the mud in the bottom.

"That's it, that's it," he nodded.

He didn't think the riders would stick to the water very long, but Allen wasn't sure. He took Lily down the stream a bit, scanning for the point where the horsemen left the stream.

On he went, trying to move as quietly as possible, because he believed that the cave might be close by. The seven pines were still in view, standing on a hillock by themselves like sentries. At last, he found a spot where the water course broadened out into a tiny lake. There was another brook bubbling down from a spring on the hillside. He spotted the hoof prints run out of the water.

"The trail!" Allen blurted out and pointed, proud of copying Ike's technique correctly. Immediately he slapped his hand over his mouth, cursing his stupidity. He stood, frozen in that silly position, until he was positive nobody heard him. He whispered to Lily in satisfaction. "And I reckon we are getting close to the end on it too."

He climbed into the saddle and they followed the trail up to where a wall of rocks arose, standing boldly out from the foothills and facing the seven pines. Allen reined in, then checked the area.

"If I ain't mistaken there's a cave over yonder," Allen said softly. He stroked his horse's neck. "Lily, if you ever had the ability to walk on tiptoes, now's the time to do it."

They moved ahead, Allen holding his weapon at the ready. Two minutes later, they turned a corner and came in sight of a large opening in the cliff side. To the right of the opening, two horses stood tethered under some trees, possibly indicating two people inside. He heard a noise.

Somebody was coming outside. He dismounted and led Lily behind some tall bushes and brush. He waited, breath held. From his vantage point, Allen could only see the person's feet as they walked by: it was a woman. She left the cave and passed them, an empty water bucket dangling from one hand, apparently bound for the spring.

That must be Nodley's wife Slavin mentioned, thought Allen. He debated about capturing her, but decided against it. He still didn't know what the situation was inside and certainly didn't want her to call out a warning to anybody else who happened to be in there.

Presently the woman came back, the bucket full of water splashing a little over the side, slapping down on the dirt. She entered the cave without looking around her. Tying up his horse, Allen crept to the entrance to the cave and peeked in.

For the moment he couldn't see well, since there was only a low fire burning in the cavern. The interior seemed to consist of multiple rooms. In the back, there was an opening angling off to the left. The front section was empty. Allen slipped inside the cave, keeping his back against one wall.

A wire grate, with a skillet on top, rested over the fire. Lying next to it was an open bedroll. Cans of food were stacked against the far side of the cavern.

"All the comforts of home," Allen said under his breath.

"Well, I have a gentleman caller," a voice said.

Allen spun around, gun ready. The woman stood in the opening in the rear wall. Her hair was dirty blonde, and the gingham dress clung to her slim figure. She once could have been described as beautiful, but the effects of a hard life were etched on her face. Even so, she still would be the center of attention as she sashayed down the street on a Saturday night. Her smile, knowing and predatory, was filled with a million stories that Allen would never hear and she would never tell. She didn't appear nervous at all with a gun aimed at her, as though it was a common occurrence.

"Stand still," Allen ordered, "don't move."

"Why, those are the same things, bless your heart," the woman placed her hands on her hips. She appraised Allen as if he was horseflesh. "My, you are a handsome young lad."

She slowly started forward, hips swinging seductively.

"I said stand still!" Allen repeated.

"Don't worry, darlin'. I'm just gettin' a closer look at the merchandise." Her laugh was light and alluring. She sidled up to the other side of the fire. She looked Allen up and down, then nodded with approval. "I'd like to see you stripped buck naked. I bet you look good ... lots of muscles ... big, strappin' ones. Ones that could squeeze a woman like me nice and tight through a long, cold night."

Even in the dimness of the cave, Allen thought he noticed speckles of gold in the green of her eyes. He felt hypnotized as she gazed back at him and he forgot to breathe. He opened his mouth to say something. Nothing came out.

"You must make your gal happy," the woman cooed.

"I don't have one." Allen wanted to sound firm and nonchalant, but his voice came out stammering and plaintive.

"No? That must be plenty disappointin' to a strong, young good lookin' fella like you." The woman tossed her head. She smiled and tilted her chin down, gazing at him from the corners of her eyes. She twisted a strand of her hair with two fingers and a thumb. "You're a regular belvidere, and yet all by yourself. Sad and lonely ... and so, so unnecessary."

Allen's grip loosened on his gun. He tightened it and cleared his throat. "I'm not here to—"

"What a cryin' shame. No mare for the stallion ... for such a wild, powerful one like you." Her voice dropped to a throaty purr. "I break stallions ... curry the kinks out. I can make a boy a man. That's a wide-open offer, darlin'." She undid the top button of her dress, the second one, then the third. Allen became distracted as he watched, feeling desire stir in him. "Well, what are you waitin' for, stallion?" She giggled. "Maybe you want me to undress you like your momma did. Some men folk do."

The woman wrapped her foot under the grate and heaved the contraption in the young rancher's direction. He hopped backward from the hot skillet, and let the grease splatter on his boots. Then, with a wild cry, she charged towards him, jumping over the fire and barreled at Allen. She grabbed his wrists and pinned him up against the cave wall. The woman bit Allen's right hand, drawing blood. He cried out and dropped his gun. She slashed at him with her other hand, scratching his face before he managed to shove her out of the way. She quickly regained her bAllence and kicked him hard in the groin. Allen doubled over with a groan.

"How's it feel, stallion? Is it like you expected?" Her cruel laughter echoed throughout the cave.

She picked up the gun, and Allen lunged at her. They crashed to the ground, and the two wrestled for control of the weapon. It felt as if Allen was taking on the wolverine once more, as her teeth sank into his arm.

The woman grabbed a can of food and bashed it against the side of Allen's head, and then she did it again. After the third time, Allen released his grip.

The woman jumped up and bounded for the cave entrance. Allen twisted around and picked up the gun.

"Stop!" he shouted.

He aimed at her and then lowered the weapon. He didn't want to shoot at a woman, but still ...

Allen fired and missed. He got to his feet and scrambled after her. The woman was already on one of the horses by the time he made it outside.

"Halt!"

"Not likely, stallion!" the woman yelled back. She whipped the horse and galloped away on a different trail than the one used by Allen, her laugh the cackle of a harpy echoing off the rocks.

He took another shot, but she rode out of sight among the trees.

"Well, she didn't count, anyhow," he told himself as he holstered his gun.

Another voice barely reached him from the cave's dim reaches, tired and weak. "Hello? Hello?"

Allen recognized it. "Uncle Barnaby?"

He raced into the cave, toward the opening in the back.

"Uncle Barnaby!" Allen called out.

"Here!" came the response.

Allen ducked his head and stepped into a narrow passage. The rough stone scraped at his back, leaving a burning sensation in its wake. He squeezed past the rock-cut wall and entered another room. The air smelled of dirt and metal. Tied to a projecting rock was an older man. His face was pale and haggard, showing he had suffered much during his confinement. Allen dashed forward.

"Uncle Barnaby! I am glad that I've found you!" he cried loudly.

"Who is that?" The prisoner awkwardly got up from where he was resting. "Allen!"

"Yes, uncle! Are you not glad to see me?" Allen knew that was a dumb thing to say, but it was the only thing he could think of in his excitement.

"Glad is not a strong enough word, my boy!" was the reply from Barnaby Winthrup, and as soon as Allen had released him he caught his nephew in his arms. "I prayed to be rescued."

"You have not been treated well. That is clear." Allen assisted his uncle to sit.

"They have used me worse than a dog, Allen. They wanted to get my secret from me. They tried to starve me into submission, feeding me only the least amount of food necessary to keep me alive."

"But they did not succeed, did they?" Allen said.

"No," Uncle Barnaby said proudly. "I told them I would die rather than allow the scoundrels to get rich through my effort."

Allen glanced around. "Do you think you can travel, uncle? I don't want to be around if that woman comes back with some of her gang. We'd be trapped in here. We need to put as much distance between us and this place before it gets too dark."

Uncle Barnaby nodded. "I can ride. Just help me to a horse."

"Good." Allen helped his uncle to his feet, wrapping an arm around his shoulder to support him as he walked. "Let's go back to the ranch. Paul and Chet will be happy to see you."

Chapter 18

Paul and Chet's second day of being prisoners on their own property looked much like the first one inside the tool shed. Their captors had lifted their arms, bound their wrists together and secured them to a roof rafter. The brothers ached from their blows and bore bruises and cuts, as well as pinpoints of burns where Mangle and Nodley poked them with the tips of hot knives as their final act yesterday before Grady called them away for something else. Neither had water nor food since on the way to the ranch.

The two didn't speak to each other, but the same questions kept running through Paul's mind, and he was sure, Chet's as well: where were Dottery and the sheriff? Why hadn't they come yet?

Paul waited for the light, but feared the sunrise, wishing for its warmth but also dreading its arrival. His desire for escape increased with every minute of darkness that he stood waiting with his brother, and his anxiety grew as the daylight brightened.

He had spent hours yesterday resisting Mangle and Nodley, who were determined to make him cower, to force him to plead with them to stop, to manipulate him into groveling before them. They didn't succeed. Paul was exhausted, but he had no doubt that they would be back this morning, and he was keenly aware that Chet was relying on him to be strong, although he was proud on how well his little brother held up. He didn't know how much more he could take of their abuse, but the alternative didn't appear any better.

Mangle, Grady, and Nodley started laughing in the morning, like roosters greeting the dawn. Paul wondered what they found funny: what they had already done to him and Chet, or what they were planning to do. He clenched his stomach in fear whenever he heard the front door creak or the sound of their footsteps in the dirt on their way to the tool shed. When they came close, he bit back a whimper. However, they turned and went back towards the house, making Paul wonder if he simply imagined them coming closer and doing nothing to him, or it was an exquisite form of torture.

Hours later, the tool shed door actually opened. Paul sucked in his breath and Chet gasped. Mangle stood in the doorway, with Nodley behind, holding a rope and his gun.

Mangle came up to Paul. "Captain Grady wants to see you."

He cut Paul loose from the roof rafter, but left his hands bound. He shoved Paul outside and gestured toward the house. Paul walked forward, Mangle and Nodley following.

Paul was terrified, but he couldn't let that overwhelm him. That wasn't logical. He decided he must face whatever was about to occur with his intellect, not by letting his emotions stampede him. He escaped from the cave that way, and now he had to control his reactions to this meeting with Grady in the same manner. It was the only way he'd survive; he was sure of that.

The three entered the main room of the house. Mangle shoved Paul toward the chair and he sat. Nodley took the rope and wrapped it several times tightly around Paul's chest, pinning his arms to his sides as well as lashing him to the chair.

"He's here, boss," Mangle called to the closed door of what was Allen's room before he and Nodley left.

Paul took a few deep breaths, at least as far as his bonds would allow, and waited. He reached inside himself, digging down as deep as he could, drawing on whatever strength remained in the well.

After a few minutes, Grady entered the room. He planted himself in front of Paul, arms crossed, and glared at the youth in the chair.

"We have some business to a-finish, you an' I." Grady spoke in a low, intense voice.

Paul didn't say anything.

"I'm talkin' to you, boy!" Grady bellowed.

"What is that?" Paul responded after a hesitation.

"We need to a-finish a lesson in showin' respect." Grady leaned over Paul, placing one hand on the chair back. He whispered. "What am I called, young savage?"

"A cheat and a liar," Paul replied.

Grady reared back and roared in wordless anger. He slapped Paul across the mouth; his vision briefly bleached white.

"I'm slapped a lot in this room," Paul muttered.

"I can see you get more, youngster," The captain grabbed Paul's hair and jerked his head back. "What's my title? What am I called? You know it. Say it."

"No."

"Say it! Captain!" Grady dictated. "You will show respect!"

"Respect is earned," Paul retorted.

Grady thrust his index finger into Paul's face and snarled, "That's where yer wrong, young savage. Respect is bought!"

The captain released Paul's hair and stalked across the room, emphasizing his words with chopping motions with his hands. "Bought! Like cattle, like land," he swung around to face Paul, "like people. Bought!"

"You can't buy people like cattle anymore."

"Don't be a fool, boy! Everybody is for sale!" Grady spat out with contempt. "When I was a young, I was dirt poor. I worked long hours in a saloon, cleanin' out spittoons. The barflies reckoned it was funny to dump disgustin' things in 'em, or do disgustin' things in 'em, an' laugh when I had to clean 'em out. They'd pour beer on my head. Throw up on the floor and call 'boy ... boy... mop this up, boy,' then spit on me when I bent over to do it. And they'd laugh and laugh ... *at me*. I were the same to 'em than what lay in the bottom of those spittoons."

Grady moved back to Paul, eyes burning with resentment. "But when the cattle baron came, 'twas all different. All those barflies, they all turned into regular boot lickers when the big sugar walked in. Every last one of 'em! He possessed lots o' land, a large herd, and money. That got him respect."

"There could be other reasons."

"No there ain't none, youngster! And it didn't take me long to figure it out!" Grady hollered. He counted off on his fingers. "Get land, get money, get respect. One follows t'other, like day follows night. I decided that was for me! No matter how, I'm getting my fair share of that kind o' respect. Then *I* would spit on *'em* and nobody would spit on me ever again. I wouldn't have to take it anymore … and 'specillay not from a half-naked young savage."

"Not everyone can be bought," Paul stated.

Grady flashed a smug, superior smile. "No?" He walked into the kitchen and in a second returned with a canteen. He dangled it in front of Paul. "You ain't had any water for a day or so. Thirsty?"

Automatically, Paul's tongue ran over his dry lips. "Of course I am."

"Well, you know the price for a refeshin' drink of water." Grady slowly moved the canteen closer.

Paul shook his head.

Grady sloshed the contents of the canteen. The liquid whispered sweetly. "A small price … just one word. It won't cost much."

"Only my self-respect."

"Self-respect!" Grady spat out the word as though it was rancid meat. "That don't exist, boy, nowhere in the entire world. Respect only comes from others. Come on. Be smart… like me."

"I am not smart," Paul said, adding with a hint of sarcasm, "like you."

Grady slapped Paul a second time. "Only one word."

Paul gathered all his strength and shouted. "No! Not from me! Ever! Not for somebody like you!"

With a quick, angry intake of breath, Grady prepared to hurl the canteen at Paul. He stopped. A sly smile crept spread across his face, as if the thought had just occurred to him of how to swat a particularly annoying fly. "Your little brother? He's thirsty too?"

"Of course he is," Paul answered quickly, with some irritation, and immediately regretted it. What was Grady up to?

"Are you noble, young savage?" the captain poised.

The question threw Paul for a moment. He didn't expect it, and he couldn't understand the reason for it. "What?"

"It means possessin' very good qualities," Grady smirked.

"I know what it means."

"Good. I didn't want to confuse you," the captain retorted acidly. "So I asks again: are you a noble savage?"

Paul's thoughts churned, trying to figure out where this was leading to and how to try to move in front of it. He answered carefully. "I believe so."

The captain could hardly contain his glee as the trap closed. "Well, my noble half-naked young savage, what will it be? Stay stubborn and proud ... keep your so-called 'self-respect' ... over a single, simple word? Or be noble and help your little brother instead? You know the price for this water for Chet ... and what you can be bought for."

Paul dropped his chin on his chest. Grady won, of all people. "Captain."

"I didn't hear that," Grady said in mock politeness, tugging on one ear. "Say it again. Louder."

Paul swallowed and looked up. "Please give the water to Chet, Captain Grady."

"See? A-doing that ain't that hard. Saul!" Grady called out. When Mangle came in, the captain handed him the canteen. "Give a drink to the monkey."

Mangle nodded and left. Grady put his fists on his hips and grinned in triumph. "Understand, boy? You ain't a-special. Everybody thinks they are, but only a few truly are."

"Like you?"

Grady smiled and jerked one thumb toward himself. "Like me. A captain among mere foot soldiers. Oh, you can feel a-special and noble 'cause you helped your brother ... but it comes with a cost. Your 'self-respect.' Respect can be bought. Remember that, boy, everybody has a price. Everybody."

"No matter how," Paul said softly.

The captain leaned forward. "What? What did you say?"

Paul met the captain's gaze, then spat in his face. With a bellow, Grady raised his hand to deliver another blow.

Chapter 19

Chet greedily drank the water from the canteen held to his lips, the cold liquid rushing down his throat. When he was finished, he heard the sound of someone beating Paul, and his cries, carried from the house.

"What are he doing to him?" Chet demanded.

"Why, nothin', monkey, nothin' at all," Mangle smiled. "Your brother and the captain are havin' a nice, friendly palaver, that's all."

Nodley appeared behind Mangle and spoke quietly. A look of alarm crossed Mangle's face. He stepped out the shed and slammed the door. Chet listened to them hurry inside the house, followed by an explosion of curses from Grady.

A few minutes later, the sound of something being dragged reached Chet's prison. The door opened, and Paul stood, propped up by Mangle. Chet's brother was barely conscious. His face was red and puffy, blood trickled from one corner of his mouth and his upper lip was split.

Mangle threw Paul to the floor and bound his hands behind his back, then crossed his ankles and tied them together. Standing,

Mangle wedged the point of his knife under Chet's chin. "You and your brother keep real quiet now. If either of you makes a sound, I'll slice you up with this blade. It'll take you eight hours to die." Stepping out, Mangle slammed the door.

"Paul... Paul," Chet whispered, "are you all right?"

A moan was the only answer.

Activity took place outside: hurried footsteps and hushed orders, followed by more footfalls and silence. Chet strained to hear more. Right before he was going to give up, he heard the hoof beats of two approaching horses. Whose were they?

Perhaps the sheriff is coming, Chet hoped.

He made out some voices, still too far away to understand the words. Chet concentrated and recognized one speaker: Allen. A second later, he knew the other one: Uncle Barnaby. They were riding into a trap.

Despite Mangle's threat, Chet opened his mouth to warn them. Before he could, gunshots rang out, mingled with a confusion of voices shouting orders and the whinnying of horses. All grew quiet for several seconds, then came the sound of a group of men walking into the house, followed by the slamming of the door.

"What's happening?" Paul mumbled. He closed his eyes and shook his head, as if to clear it.

"Are you all right?" Chet asked.

"I've felt better, but yeah, yeah, I think so," Paul took a deep breath. "I just wish my ears would stop ringing. There was shooting ..."

"Allen and Uncle Barnaby are back."

"What!" Paul struggled to sit up.

"Mangle and Nodley bushwhacked them, and everybody has gone inside the house," Chet reported.

"Are Allen and Uncle hurt?"

Chet shook his head. "I'm not sure. I don't think so."

"Wait! Somebody's coming," Paul hissed.

The shed door was flung open. Allen and Captain Grady stood framed in the doorway. Mangle was just behind them.

"Allen!" Chet and Paul cried out.

Allen gazed at his brothers with eyes full of guilt. His voice was sad. "You two look like you've been through hell."

"An' unless Barnaby Winthrup tells me what I want to know," Grady threatened, "they will be a-making another visit, pickin' up with the young savage here, all the while yer uncle watches."

"No." Allen said firmly. He turned to the captain. "They've suffered enough. Leave them alone." He tapped himself on his chest. "Me. If you do anything, do it to me."

"Allen, no," Paul exclaimed.

Allen twisted toward his younger brother and barked, "Shut up!" He faced Grady. "Well?"

Grady thought for a second as he stared at Allen with cold, calculating eyes, and shrugged. "You'll do."

The door closed again. It seemed as if the three split up: two moved towards the barn, one went to the house. After a few minutes, another group left the house and went to the barn. An alarmed shout from Uncle Barnaby reached Chet.

"Allen!"

At once an argument broke out between Allen and Uncle Barnaby. They began shouting at one another, their irate voices rising out of the barn, but Chet couldn't make out the words. The angry discussion ended with the crack of a whip and a scream from Allen, followed by another, then another, then another.

"They're whipping him," Paul said hoarsely.

A second exclamation came from Uncle Barnaby. "Stop!"

"No, Uncle!" yelled Allen, "don't tell—"

Another snap and a yelp of pain cut off the sentence. The blows fell faster until Allen's screams turned into grunting groans. Chet made himself not to count the strokes as they went on.

"Stop! Stop it now! You win! Please!" Uncle Barnaby pleaded loudly.

Quiet blanketed everything again. Chet strained to listen. "What's going on?"

"Can I see out through walls?" Paul snapped.

The answer came shortly, in the sound of several horses ridden away from the ranch. A deadly stillness fell, punctuated by bird songs which seem to mock the brothers.

Paul struggled futilely against his bindings. He stopped, out of breath. "We've got to get out of here before they return. If they do, that is."

"You don't think Grady would leave us here to starve to death, do you?" asked Chet.

"Four unmarked graves on the prairie mean nothing to a man like him," Paul fought to free himself again. "I need something to slice these ropes, but Grady left nothing in here."

"Wait! There is now!" Chet tilted his head toward one wall, full of bullet holes from the wild shooting yesterday. "I patched a hole last week with the top from a tin can. See? Way down, near the floor. One of Mangle's shots struck the edge of it and bent it away from the wood. I remember that lid was sharp. I had to be careful not to cut myself."

"I understand!" Paul wriggled and rolled over to the hole. He hoisted himself into position until he felt the part of the lid contact the rope. He moved his arms up and down as much as he could, a faint sound of the sharp edge sawing back and forth seemingly filling the shed. Minutes crept by, and Paul stopped.

"I'm getting cramped," he breathed out. He rested for a few seconds, then resumed his work. "This is harder than it looks."

"You can do it," Chet encouraged his older brother.

Perspiration beaded on Paul's forehead as he panted from the exertion. Suddenly, he gasped. "It's coming! I felt my hands move!"

"Keep going! You're almost through!"

Paul hunched his shoulders together and forced his elbows out, and pulled against the frayed rope. He stopped and shook his head. "No...no good. I can't."

"Once more, Paul," Chet urged, "Try! Twist your wrists. You're almost free!"

Paul nodded and took a deep breath. He clenched his teeth and tried again. His hands flew apart.

The brothers laughed in relief. Paul removed the binding from around his feet, and got up, steadying himself against the wall. He lurched over to Chet.

"Stand on your toes," he instructed Chet. "Lessen the tension off the rope."

Chet did so, and Paul untied him. The two stood for a moment, rubbing their wrists, before they moved toward the door. It wouldn't open.

Chet peered between the boards. "They jammed a plank under the handle."

"All right, Chet, you and I against that door," Paul said determinedly. He stepped a couple of feet away and turned sideways to his target. Chet joined him. "Now!"

The two crashed into the door at the same time. It shuddered, but remained firm. They backed up and smashed into the wood again. The door bent a little.

"Every time we hit it, I think the door shoves the plank deeper into the ground," sighed Paul. He examined the frame and thought a moment. "Maybe we should try the hinge side. The screws may let loose." Chet nodded in agreement, and the two took up different positions. "Go!"

There was a splintering of breaking wood, and a sharper sound of snapping metal. The upper hinge had given way, and the top of the door hung open a crack.

"This last time should do it," Paul said, massaging his sore shoulder. "Ready?"

"You bet."

"Make it count. One ... two ... three ... now!"

The brothers ran into the door with all the force they could muster. The lower hinges pulled out, and the door flew out of the doorway as if it had been blasted by a charge of explosive. Chet and Paul spilled out of the opening on the dirt, their momentum keeping them moving forward on all fours. They regained their footing and raced to the barn.

"Allen!"

Allen sat back on his knees, wrists tied around the other side of a post and his forehead resting against it. Red, angry welts, moist with sweat and blood, crisscrossed his bare back. He lifted his head at their voices. "Chet? Paul?"

Paul freed his older brother's hands from the rope as Chet helped him to his feet. Allen stood, swaying slightly. He took a deep breath, winced with pain, then started to look around.

"I've got to go after Uncle Barnaby," Allen mumbled. "I can't lose him again. Where's my shirt?" He scooped it off the ground and turned toward his horse, still saddled but in her stall.

"Don't let him leave, Chet," Paul crisply ordered.

Chet blocked Allen's path and yanked the shirt out of his hand. Allen pulled back, but Chet hung on. The older brother seemed to be angry, and his features twisted into an annoyed appearance. He tried to take the garment back again, but Chet wouldn't give it up.

Slapping his thigh with the flat of his hand, Allen growled and stepped to one side. Chet countered it. Allen moved the other direction, only to have the youngest brother bar his way again. Allen attempted to push him out of the way, but Chet remained rooted. His stance widened, feet shoulder-width apart, hands raised to shoulder height, palms out to Allen, fingers splayed.

"What the hell—" Allen fumed. He raised one hand.

"Are you going to strike me like you did Paul?" Chet asked in an even tone.

A flash of shame crossed Allen's face. He shook his head and dropped his fist.

Paul came behind Chet. "I know trying to stop you going after Uncle Barnaby is impossible, but I need to at least take care of your back as good as I can. I don't want you becoming feverish and falling off your horse."

"But they're getting away!" Allen protested.

"There are four riders. They will leave an obvious trail," Paul replied simply. "Chet, go to the pile of our stuff and pull out a chair, and have Allen straddle it. Find a couple of crashes, too."

Paul stepped out of the barn. Allen swore under his breath and again tried to get to his horse. Chet grabbed on his wrists like handcuffs.

"What is this?" Allen fought against Chet's grip. "Are you two giving *me* orders?"

"Yes," Chet asserted. "You're going to do what Paul said. You know it is best for you."

Allen worked to break Chet's hold again, but he was no match for his brother's strength. Allen struggled for a second longer, then a look of resignation crossed his face. He nodded.

Chet released Allen, and the two went outside. Finding a chair, Chet pointed at it. His older brother swung a leg over the seat and sat backwards. Paul came out of the house carrying a bowl of water while Chet fished through their belongings and pulled out two linen crashes.

"Luckily, Grady kept water heating on the stove," Paul placed the bowl next to Allen, and took one of the crashes from Chet and soaked it in the water. "Allen, this is going to hurt, maybe more than the actual flogging itself." He spoke to the younger brother. "Keep him in that chair."

"Go ahead and curse, holler and cry," Chet told Allen, "you don't have to prove anything to us."

Allen's eyes angrily snapped up to meet Chet's, but the expression melted into gratitude. Chet pressed down on Allen's shoulders.

"Ready?" asked Paul.

Grabbing hold of Chet's forearms, Allen took a deep breath and nodded. He cursed, hollered and cried as Paul began to clean the back wounds with one of the linens. When Paul finished, he pinned another crash around his brother's torso.

"All right," Paul said, "I've done what I could, but we need to get you to a doctor soon."

Allen let go of Chet, inhaled a few times, and stood. Grimacing in pain, he shrugged on his shirt and headed toward the house. "Guns?"

"Still in the rack," Paul replied. "Allen ... "

Allen stopped and turned back.

"You took that whipping for me," Paul said. "I didn't have the strength to stand up under it. Thank you."

There was a silent pause.

"Thank you ... " Allen's voice was heavy with emotion. He cleared his throat. "Thank you for the doctoring. And thank you for making me stay, Chet."

"Of course. We take care of each other. We watch out for each other," Paul said.

"It's what brothers do," added Chet.

Allen glanced between Paul and Chet, almost as if seeing them for the first time. A broad grin broke out on his face. Chet saw his brother, the brother he knew before Pa died, reappear.

"All grown up," Allen said quietly. He looked away, cleared his throat again and sniffed a couple of times. After a second, he took a deep breath and continued toward the house. He stopped on the porch and faced his siblings.

"Well, what are you two waiting for? Get yourselves ready. I need your help," Allen said sharply. He smiled again. "It's what brothers do."

Chapter 20

Allen readied their horses, loading rifles into the scabbards and additional ammunition into the saddlebags. Meanwhile, Chet and Paul cleaned up and changed into fresh clothes, each managing to chew on some jerked meat as they climbed on their mounts. In about an hour, the brothers started after Uncle Barnaby, Grady, Mangle and Nodley. After a short while, the hoof prints left the main road.

"You were right, Paul," remarked Allen, "this is an easy trail to follow."

"They didn't expect to be followed," replied Paul.

A distant hail reached them. They turned in their saddles and looked behind them. Three horsemen were in the distance.

"It's Mister Dottery, Blowfen, and the sheriff," Paul said. "I'll ride back and tell them the situation. You two keep going. I'll catch up."

Paul spurred his horse, and galloped toward the other riders, his path marked by puffs of dust drifting into the air, breaking the sun into shafts of light. In about five minutes, he returned to Allen and Chet.

"I asked them to watch the house and lock up those documents," Paul reported. "We don't know how many more men are in Grady's gang. Once they've done that, they will follow us, at least the sheriff will. I reckoned we'd want to finish this matter on our own, if we can."

"If!" exclaimed Chet. "There ain't no 'if' about it!"

Allen nodded in approval. "Good thinking, Paul."

The boys rode on in silence for a while.

"Did Uncle Barnaby tell you anymore about his claim?" Chet asked.

Allen shook his head. "Not a thing, no matter how much I asked. He said he didn't want to put us in a position where somebody might do us harm to get the information."

"Well, that didn't work out so well," Paul commented dryly.

Chet and Allen chuckled.

"So he said nothing, no clue of any kind?" Chet persisted.

"Perhaps one," Allen said after some thought. "Before everybody left the barn, Uncle Barnaby mentioned 'Wedding Cake Rock' several times. Loudly, like he wanted to make sure I understood it."

"Wedding Cake Rock?" Chet asked, puzzled.

Allen nodded. "At least, I think that was what he said. To be honest, after the whipping, the pain could have clouded my mind."

"Wedding Cake Rock," Chet rolled the name around in his mouth. "I don't recollect every hearing of such a place. Have you, Paul?"

Paul shook his head. "I draw a blank."

The tracks they followed led up into the second foothills. The weather turned rather gloomy, but the three boys didn't mind.

"It's better than being so raging hot," noted Paul. "My head aches when I ride and it's so hot."

"If it only doesn't rain," said Chet. "We can always use it, goodness knows, but after that last storm, I hope it holds off at least for twenty-four hours."

"I doubt if it will come just yet. It hasn't threatened long enough," Allen checked overhead.

As they continued, the sky blackened with clouds. Chet happened to glance across the plains below. He pointed. "Paul! What is that?"

The three reined in their horses, their attention drawn to a round, black cloud on the horizon to the east. It was hardly a yard in diameter, apparently, when first seen, but it increased in size rapidly.

It was moving directly toward them, and in less than two minutes from the time Chet uttered his cry the cloud had covered fully a third of the distance.

"From what I have read, I think that is a cyclone cloud," Paul said thoughtfully. "And still—"

"That's exactly what it is, Paul," Allen confirmed.

"Who ever heard of a cyclone up here among the foothills?" returned Chet. "I didn't believe they ever strike this territory."

"Maybe it got lost," Paul gave a wry grin. "I didn't think they formed in this area, but still, cyclones are erratic things at the best."

"We've had them here before, Paul, but not often," responded Allen. "The last one I remember around here was about a dozen years ago, when you two were babies."

"It seems as if the thing is coming this way," Chet said uneasily.

"Look!" Paul pointed. "A tail is dropping down from the cloud. Fascinating!"

"I hate to end your observation, Paul, but I reckon the best thing we can do is to make tracks for some place of safety," Allen said.

"That's true," agreed Chet. "Come on!"

The three started up the trail at a fast trot, with Paul twisted backwards to keep his eyes on the unusual sight. Only a hundred feet of the distance had been covered when a strange rush and roar of wind filled the air.

"Here it comes!" warned Paul.

"Quick, Chet, Paul," Allen yelled over the howl of the gale, "down into that hollow before it strikes us!"

Allen plunged into the basin, which was six to eight feet below the level of the trail and not over ten yards in diameter. Chet and Paul followed, ducking as they did so, for already dirt and flying branches filled the air.

"None too soon!" Paul slid off his saddle.

"Get the horses down!" Allen ordered.

Between the three of them, they managed to get the animals to lie down close to a wall of the hollow. The brothers huddled near, hanging on their horses' bridles, waiting almost breathlessly. The noise increased, sounding like thousands of buffalo stampeding just overhead.

Chet's ears popped, then tremendous pressure began building up in his head. His eardrums felt as if they were going to burst. He screamed at the pain. His breath seemed to be sucked out of his lungs. Dirt, rocks, branches fired in on the trio, almost as if shot from a cannon. With a great snapping crash, a pine tree toppled over the top of the basin, blocking the opening. Smells of rain and fresh cut wood flowed over the group.

Rush, whinnying in panic, tried to rise. "Stay down, Rush, stay down, boy," Chet held down on the bridle with all his strength, gritting his teeth.

Then came an eerie silence. Chet's ears stopped hurting, and he took huge gulps of air. From what sounded like far away, Allen's voice reached him.

"Is everybody all right? Chet? Paul?"

"I'm fine," Chet called back. A second later, Paul did the same.

The cyclone was short and sharp. From the time it first struck the foothills until the time it spent itself in the distance was barely four minutes. Chet sat up, dirt rolling off him like water, his neck scratched from the impact of several pointed sticks and stones. He examined the green roof over the hollow.

"Here's an opening between the branches," Chet said. He squeezed through the gap and pulled himself out of the hole. He looked around and gasped.

From where he stood, stretching down to the plains, many trees were literally torn up by the roots, and brush was leveled as if cut by a mowing machine. Dirt and pebbles which had been perhaps carried for miles were deposited here, there, and everywhere. Damage was less where Chet was, but even here, branches were ripped off, and several smaller trees, like the one covering their refugee, had blown down.

Paul joined his brother. "That is the kind of adventure I never want to experience again."

"Nor do I," put in Chet.

"It was a full-fledged cyclone and no mistake," Allen said as he climbed out of the hollow and surveyed the scene. "Had that struck a town it would have razed every building in it."

"A storm like that can do more damage than can be repaired in ten years," observed Chet. "I wonder where it started from?"

"Somewhere out on the flat lands near the river, I reckon," guessed Paul.

"We must help the horses out," said Chet. "Poor things!"

Chet, Allen and Paul, using all their strength, raised up one end of the tree, and shifted it off the hole. Their animals were frightened still, so the brothers led them out instead of riding them. Allen walked a few steps back in the direction they had come and searched the ground.

"It looks as if the wind swept the very trail away! I can't see anything of it ahead. Nothing. Even the heavens themselves are against us!" Allen railed. He clenched his fists and bellowed in frustration. He dropped his fists to his sides, his head sagging to his chest.

Chet walked up to him and placed his hand on his arm. "We'll figure something out, Allen. Nothing can stop the Winthrups when we put our mind to something."

"Not even a cyclone?" Allen asked bitterly.

"Not even a cyclone," Chet answered.

Allen gave his younger brother a weary smile.

Suddenly Paul called out: "Of course! Why didn't I think of that before!"

He wasn't talking to his brothers, but rather stood a little distance away, facing the mountains. He turned around and rushed up to Chet and Allen. "Wedding Cake Rock! Wedding Cake

Rock!" He took a deep breath, as if having difficulty controlling thoughts crowding his brain. "What does a wedding cake look like?"

"Paul, what does that have—" Allen started.

"No, no, wait," Paul held out his hand. "What does a wedding cake look like?"

Chet pictured one in his mind. "Well, it is tall ... has layers ... "

"You're right! Layers! A wedding cake is made up of layers! Like sedimentary rock!" Paul proclaimed. He glanced between his brothers. "Savvy?"

"Sedimentary rock?" Allen shrugged. "What is that?"

"Rock in layers," Paul explained, demonstrating with his hands, "different rocks, one layer stacked on top of the other. Like a cake."

"But ... " Chet began, confused.

"Allen ... Allen ... " Paul again paused in his excitement to take a breath, "did you tell Uncle Barnaby about my experience at Black Rock River?"

"Why, yes, certainly. He wanted to know everything that happened during his captivity, but what... " Allen appeared puzzled.

"I was in his mine!" Paul said. He grabbed Allen by his arms. "I saw veins of what I thought was quartz or fool's gold. Since I don't understand much about prospecting and had other things on my mind at the time, like finding my way out of there, I didn't pay any much attention to it, but it probably was the real thing. When I finally crawled outside, I emerged next to a tall outcropping made up of layers of rock—sedimentary rock: Wedding Cake Rock! Don't you see? Uncle Barnaby was trying to tell you where they were heading, but in such a way that Grady wouldn't pick up on it."

Allen opened his mouth to say something, but Paul pulled away and pointed to a peak. "Do you see that mountain? You can see it clearly now that the pine has fallen, and some other branches are down. I thought it looked familiar. I climbed that summit to find my bearings after getting out of the cave. Uncle could have meant that Wedding Cake Rock is around its base," Paul scanned the area, and jabbed his index finger toward a spot. "Over there. If the others are going around the mountain to reach the same spot, we can cut across here and arrive first!"

The eldest brother rubbed the back of one hand across his chin. "I don't know. If we check ahead, we could pick up the trail again …"

"Or not," Paul stressed.

Allen checked the terrain leading toward the peak and shook his head doubtfully. "That's rough country to ride over."

"We take the horses as far as we can, then hike the rest of the way," Paul said.

"No, too chancy. We could most likely pick up the trail again on the other side of the debris. My decision is to go—" Allen stopped as though something occurred to him. He looked at Chet. "What do you think we should do?"

Chet hesitated. His older brother never asked his opinion before, especially as a tie breaker. Finally, he spoke. "I agree with Paul."

Allen glanced several times between the place Paul indicated and where the trail they were following once headed, seemingly appraising the situation. He addressed Paul. "Take the lead."

Chapter 21

The three climbed on their horses with Paul in front, followed by Allen and Chet. They started toward the mountain peak. At first, their path was almost impassable in spots, and more than once had to make a wide detour to avoid fallen tree branches and gathered brush. The terrain struck an upward course with the trio threading their way through trees and boulders. The slope sharply steepened, leading to a split between the rocks.

"Be careful here," Paul cautioned. "This could be a mighty slippery spot for the best of horses."

Scarcely had he spoken when Rush slipped to his knees, pitching Chet to the ground with one of his feet caught in the stirrup. He let out a cry as he fell. Rush struggled back to his feet and continued on, pulling Chet along.

"Stop Rush!" cried Paul. "If you don't, he'll bang Chet's head off!"

Before he had finished speaking, Allen jumped off Lily. He ran back and took hold of Rush by the bridle. Partly stunned, it took several seconds before Chet could recover enough to disengage his foot and stand.

"Thanks, Allen," he said.

"Are you all right?" Allen asked.

Chet rubbed the back of his skull. "Just bumped my head."

"Nothing important," Allen replied with a grin.

With a laugh, Chet climbed up on his horse. The brothers went on, the ground growing rougher and more precipitous. Paul called a halt.

"We'll have to use our own two feet from here on," he said as he dismounted. He pointed to a ridge higher up. "We're almost there."

They found a shaded, grassy area, and tethered their horses. After loading themselves up with as much ammunition as they could carry, they pulled out their Winchesters and began working their way uphill. It soon turned into a climb, as the three fought to maintain their balance with rifles in hand. They neared the top of the ridge.

"Just on the other side," Paul said as he caught his breath.

Allen scanned the area. "Let's hide behind those rocks to the left. They're on the edge of the hollow."

Crouching down, the brothers quickly arrayed themselves behind a group of boulders, providing a view of the entire bowl. They took off their hats to be less visible, and arranged their ammunition next to them.

"There's Wedding Cake Rock," Paul indicated the outcropping on the opposite side.

Allen nodded. "It looks like one, all right."

"The sage brush covers the way I got out of the cave," Paul went on, "but there must be an easier way in Uncle found. Perhaps farther along."

"Quiet!" Chet hissed.

A group of figures appeared over the far ridge: Uncle Barnaby first, with Grady, Mangle and Nodley behind. They started down the slope.

"Wait until they get to the bottom," Allen said quietly. "Fire on my command."

His brothers nodded, pulling up their rifles. Slowly, carefully, the other group worked their way down the rubble of the wall, starting miniature landslides of rocks and pebbles rattling to the ground. After what felt to be forever to Chet, the men reached the bottom. Uncle Barnaby stepped a few paces ahead of Grady and the others, waving one hand as if explaining something.

"Uncle Barnaby! Take cover!" Allen pulled up his rifle.

Their uncle dove behind a boulder. Surprised, the other men drew their guns and backed away.

"Fire!" Allen called to Chet and Paul.

Their three rifles erupted into fire at the same time. Grady, Mangle and Nodley shot back as they took shelter behind another group of rocks. Gunshots echoed in the hollow, and blue smoke writhed over the scene like ghosts. Sharp pings sang through the air like angry bees as bullets ricocheted off the boulders. The pungent odor of gunpowder mixed in with hot smell of pine and dirt.

"Hold your fire," Allen commanded. The boys stopped. A few minutes later, so did the other men. "This isn't getting us any-where. We have a standoff."

"I guess we'll have to wait them out," sighed Paul.

Chet crawled to Allen. "See that boulder about halfway up the side over there? I can sneak behind it, and get the drop on them from the rear. We'll trap them between you and Paul and me."

Allen shook his head. "I don't know. It doesn't seem that big."

"Neither am I."

"An awful lot of open ground lies between that rock and the lip of the ridge. If they spot you, or you even knock some pebbles loose and they pick up on that, then you have no cover. You'll be..." the eldest brother's voice drifted off.

"You and Paul just make sure they don't see me, then," Chet urged.

"I don't know... " Allen repeated.

"Let me try, Allen. Give me a chance." Chet's voice was level and earnest.

Allen gazed at Chet and nodded. His voice caught as he spoke. "Please be careful."

Chet grinned. "You don't need to worry about that, big brother."

"Paul ... " Allen started.

"I heard." Paul held aim with his rifle and squeezed off a shot. "Damn, he moved."

Chet dropped below the ridge line and began moving as fast as he could through the jumble of boulders and trees. The ground crunched underfoot, and tree branches whispered as he brushed past them. He could hear his own breathing, tense and labored. Occasionally came the sound of a gunshot when one side or the other spotted a target of opportunity.

He halted when he heard a horse's whinny. Looking down the hill, he saw Uncle Barnaby, Grady, Mangle, and Nodley's horses tethered under a tree. He was in the correct spot. He stopped and rested until he caught his breath, then started scrambling up toward the ridge.

No, stop, Chet angrily told himself, *you can't go at this like a bull at a gate as usual. This needs to be slow, steady, and above all, quiet.*

Pulling rein on himself, he began creeping as softly as he could. He reached the lip and peered over the edge. The rock he was aiming for seemed a lot smaller, and a lot farther away.

Keeping as low as he could, he started inching down the slope, cautiously testing his footing before putting his full weight on it. His heart pounded, and he realized he had been holding his breath. He exhaled; it sounded to him as loud as the cyclone. Bit by bit, he moved nearer to the boulder.

Closer ... closer ... one step after another ... almost there ...

His foot slipped, and Chet flopped backwards. He dropped his rifle, and rocks began to tumble down the slope. At the same time, Allen and Paul opened up, with Grady, Mangle and Nodley returning fire. Chet snatched his Winchester, and rolled behind the rock, expecting to feel the impact of bullets any moment. He sat with his back against it, his pulse pounding.

The gunfire died down. Chet peeked over the top of the boulder. He spotted the shoulders and heads of the other men. He aimed his rifle and fired. The shot neatly lifted Mangle's hat off his head. The outlaw spun around.

"The next one goes in your brain, Mangle!" Chet called out.

The man pulled up his revolver, and Chet fired again. Mangle grabbed his shoulder and dropped his gun.

"Sorry, I guess I missed!" Chet said. "My aim is about as lousy as yours! Maybe I'll try again!"

Paul's voice carried across the hollow. "He's right! He's a bad aim, Mangle! He'll fill you full of holes before hitting something vital!"

"Give up, Grady!" Allen shouted. "Drop your gun belts and step out from behind those rocks, hands up! Do it!" Grady, Mangle and Nodley complied with the order and stood in the open ground, looking miserable. "Uncle Barnaby?"

"Here, Allen!"

"Grab their guns and cover them until we get down there."

"With the greatest of pleasure!" Uncle Barnaby emerged from behind the boulder and headed for the weapons.

A voice boomed from behind Chet. "Ah, shoot! We missed all the fun!"

Chet grinned, turning to face Ike standing on the rim. Mr. Dottery, Blowfen, and the sheriff were next to him. "You may have missed the party, Ike, but you're in time to help clean up!"

***

"... and then that there cyclone put me and my horse down, gentle as you please, fifty mile away!" Ike stuffed another forkful of food in his mouth.

Barnaby, Paul and Chet roared with laughter. They sat around the table in the ranch house, the empty serving dishes, the remnants of one of the youngest brother's huge meals, lay piled in the center.

"Hey, now! That be the gospel truth!" Ike protested.

"The gospel according to whom?" taunted Paul.

Ike jabbed his fork at himself. "Why, me, of course!" He resumed eating. "Sure good cookin', Chet. Say Barnaby, you takin' Paul to one of 'em fancy eatin' places in Frisco when you two go?"

"Surely, Ike, but likely I'll have to rope and drag him out of Roman's Booksellers store first," Uncle Barnaby said.

"I have to something to do while you meet with Mr. Urner!" Paul spoke up.

Another round of laughter filled the room. Allen came in, taking his place at the table. He jerked his thumb toward the outside. "Mr. Dottery just made a suggestion. If Grady's ranch comes up for sale—"

"He won't be using it any more," Paul said.

Allen chuckled. "True. Anyway, if the ranch comes up for sale, Mr. Dottery says he and I should buy it together, then split the acreage fifty-fifty."

"Well, you inherit your share of this property in a few months," Uncle Barnaby said, "It's your decision. What did you tell him?"

"I told him I have to talk it over with my brothers first," Allen replied. "What you two think? Paul? Chet?"

"I say buy it," Paul responded.

"Make that two," Chet added.

"It's unanimous," Allen stated. "We'd get the southern portion. That includes the house."

"I claim it for me!" Uncle Barnaby said. "I'll move in there and let you boys run the ranch. I've never been too fond of cattle. Say, Ike, there's plenty of room in that place. Why don't you settle down?"

Ike shook his head. "'Preciate the offer, but I wander a lot. But I sure would be pleased to know I have a place to rest my head when I'm around."

"Done," said Uncle Barnaby. "There's always a room for you. And I'll make sure Chet cooks for you."

Ike beamed as he finished off his food.

"Oh, Paul," Chet hinted in a sing-song voice as he pushed his dirty plate toward his brother.

"I know, I know. I get the idea," Paul grinned. "I promised I'd wash and dry."

He stood, picked up his plate and gathered the ones used by Dottery, Blowfen, and Chet. He walked into the kitchen, then yelled. "Chet! Did you have to use every single pot we own?"

Chet laughed. "I was especially messy tonight!"

"I'll help, Paul," Allen called as he got up.

Later that evening, Allen stood on the front porch, gazing over the land. The full moon was rising over the mountains and spreading a deep blue glow over the valley. He inhaled the fresh air and let out a contented sigh. The air was dry, but as it touched his cheeks, it carried with it a hint of moisture. A slight breeze ruffled his hair as it brought with it the scent of fresh soil. Paul and Chet joined him.

"It's beautiful," Paul said softly.

Allen nodded. "It sure is." He was quiet for a moment. "We've been through a time, haven't we?"

"That we have," Paul agreed. "But we came out the other side."

"Together," Chet put in.

The trio stood in silence for a minute.

"Listen, Paul, Chet, I want to say..." Allen faltered, then continued. "I want to say how sorry I am on the way I've been acting ... it's just... I don't know... I guess I didn't reckon how hard it would be, you know, to try to replace Pa. I couldn't do it, I didn't know how and just became... I was plain too proud to ask for help."

"We understand," said Paul.

"Although at times I wanted to whack you upside the head with a board," Chet added.

"Maybe that would have helped," Allen laughed. "And if I start behaving like I used to, go ahead and whack away." He put his arms around the shoulders of his brothers. "Like you said Chet, nothing can stop us Winthrups when we're united. That's us. Brothers three."